ALPHA
(THE PREQUEL)

TO

THE SECRET BUTTERFLY SERIES™
(THE EIGHTEEN BOOKS
OF ROSEMARY)

A Novel by

Rosemary Lightfoot Ness-Bitner

To order, wherever books are sold:

ISBN: 978-1-961850-08-8 for eBook
ISBN: 978-1-961850-07-1 for Print Paperback

A caution and disclaimer

All characters, events, conversations, and acknowledgements in this book are fictional, the product of the author's imagination, or used fictitiously. Any resemblance to actual characters, living or dead, events past or present, localities, or conversations, is entirely coincidental.

If you are offended by characters' offensive behaviors and expressions of strong opinions about controversial subjects, you are advised and cautioned to not purchase this book or listen to this audio book. If you are a child under the age of eighteen, do not purchase this book or listen to this audio book as it contains erotic adult content. Sexual activity may cause diseases. If you engage in sex, please do so responsibly. If you smoke, drink, do drugs, drive a car, ride a bike, play golf, raise a child, hunt, fish, brush your teeth, cross the street, cough, sneeze, gamble, or vote, please also do those things responsibly.

The print version layout of ALPHA (THE PREQUEL) © to THE SECRET BUTTERFLY SERIES ™ was created by Andrea Reider of Reider Books. The print and audio cover design of the book was created by Carrie Spencer of Cheeky Covers. And I'm Melanie Monarch, your audio book narrator.

Appreciation:

My special recognition and thanks to the American Library Association are in order. Your efforts to prevent books from being banned is vital to sustaining freedom of speech in America. Without your vigilance and safeguards against malcontented censurers, the perspectives which my characters express regarding women's reproductive issues might never be known. Sadly, some may label my work as sociopathic, or something worse. They may call for my books to be banned. But through your noble defense of free speech, my characters' unique and valuable perspectives can be shared. And humanity will be better for it. I thank you, profusely,

Rosemary

Ode to Amygdala:

Please set me free a mig da lee
Release me from faith and race
Travails; all social tyrannies,
Tiny gland though you may be
Whisk me to my special place
Where fantasy will set me free
Your hormones, now, my mind embrace,
Control me; push away conformity
Free limbic me to kiss her face;
Leave tortured life behind me,
And cleave me to my dreaming place
Her mons will warmly welcome me
I revel in her touch, her scents and lace
Enraptured shameless artistry;
So glorious her wanton grace!
Please set me free a mig da lee
Let me know in tim a cy
In her immoral sacred place
Join our souls in revere,
Help me be my other me; Let
Release and peace sweep over me
Yes! Freed finally; completely,
Quench my lust's familiar taste
Imbibing her pornography.

Rosemary

CHAPTER ONE

DEATH PENALTY

Pornography is intimate artistry which delivers freedom from religion. (Rosemary Ness Bitner, author)

The limbic mind is extraordinary. It's capable of doing extraordinary things. Few understand it; most find it incomprehensible; yet some find ways to dwell within it. For those it is guiltless, rewarding, exhilarating and beautiful. (Rosemary Ness Bitner, author)

This time Pete wore a blue suit with white shirt and a red patterned tie. His attorney got him cleaned up for his trial. Gone were his scruffy beard, ragged jeans, and tie-dyed T shirt. Gone too, was his horrific stench.

Frank: *"He looks like his old self again. That's the Pete I know,"* commented one well-dressed businessman, seated in the courtroom's public gallery.

John: *"Surreal,"* replied his colleague. The two patrician civic leaders were pillars of their community. They had come to the courthouse to give moral support to their friend.

Frank: *"He fell so far. It's hard to believe. I'm still trying to get my head around what happened to him; but it's hard. Joyce questioned why I would even bother coming to this."*

John: *"Mandy, too. I heard her talking to Joyce on the phone about it. She's outraged. She wants to see Pete executed for what he did to Marge and their kids. I don't think any wife could understand it. Ours don't even want to try."*

The ante room door between the judge's chambers and his Bench opened. The judge's gray-haired head peered through. His steel gray eyes surveyed the huge crowd in the packed courtroom. That figured. It's not every day that a community gets to see a civic leader on trial for murder. The cold, unrevealing eyes lingered momentarily on the man seated at the defendant's table. Pete Peterson was the man whom the community and its legal system had served up for trial. The judge gritted his teeth and pinched his lips together. He knew this trial would be grim business. He tried not to think about what was about to happen: *'Just do your job,'* he reminded himself.

Thinking about the drama that was about to unfold made him feel dirty. He'd reviewed the DA's evidence at the preliminary hearing. The evidence would be gory pictures; stab wounds; severed throats; blood; bloated faces. Not just bloodied faces; horrified contorted faces caught in the terrified grasps of their impending, certain deaths. DA Coglin was skillful. He racked up convictions. Defendants feared him for good reason. He knew how to put the jurors' imaginations into the places of unfortunate victims. He knew how to shove jurors' faces into the despicable, repugnant, heinous nature of these murders. The judge knew Goglin's tactics well. Coglin would relentlessly hammer those pictures into the jurors' minds. He'd hammer hard, like he was pounding nails into their brains; making those horrifying images real and unforgettable; fixing them there; permanently. Coglin was out for blood. He would make those jurors hate Peterson with a vengeance. He wanted to take Peterson's scalp, and he wanted those jurors frenzied and cheering for him while he took it.

And after seeing the ghastly photos until they haunted them, the jurors would predictably feel sickened. They would agree that no decent person could do such a despicable thing. They would feel outraged; emotionally charged. They would agree that even the humanely administered death penalty was insufficient punishment for these heinous crimes. Only a vile, evil monster could do something as horrific as this. How could a father sever his sweet, innocent, young daughter's throat: take her life like that? And with a hunting type of knife with a serrated edge used for cutting bone, no less? The poor girl had to suffer excruciating, agonizing pain! And by her own father! She had to be horrified! Trust shattered! Cut down at the cusp of her budding young life!

That no good, dirty, rotten son of a bitch who took those precious young lives in that barbaric way would have to pay. The jurors would feel it was their moral duty to make the Defendant pay. They would want to take revenge on him. Death would not be enough punishment. He deserved to be scourged! Eyes gouged out! Bones broken! Then, after all that pain, he needed to experience death by hanging by a slow rope. Agonizing death; not the quick snap drop neck break rope from a gallows death. No. A different sort of rope. The kind of rope that slow grips the throat and suffocates; crushes the larynx slowly, painfully; and makes its victim's eyeballs bulge out; his tongue lapse free; while his legs flail uselessly in air. Even that kind of death would be too merciful for this no-good son of a bitch. But some measure of their visceral hatred would finally be assuaged. Revenge would be felt. The jurors would feel they had done something right and good, because they were descent people who were not going to tolerate some no-good son of a bitch living and walking amongst them. Yes, these jurors would deliver the perfunctory guilty verdict and they would give the court their dutiful recommendation for the death penalty.

His job, as judge, was to block off all avenues for the defense's certain appeals. He needed to make this phase of Peterson's execution neat and tidy; give it all appearances of being politely civilized and legal; make it into something that everyone could go home from, wash their hands, and feel good about the verdict of guilty and the recommended punishment of death. And, the judge reminded himself, he needed to thank these good people for their service and make them feel good about what they did. He needed to do that final bit of service to the community to help them heal from the horrible trauma that befell four of their innocent fellow citizens.

But the judge had a problem with his conscience about this case. Peterson was a rock-solid pillar of the community. He was a good man; a damn good man; an exceptional, outstanding, civic minded man. He belonged to the Rotary and Elks clubs. He'd had a stint as mayor just a few short years ago. Did it even seem remotely possible that a successful businessman; devout church goer; and respected family man like Peterson would completely lose his mind over a piece of ass? With a profligate, notorious, porn star whore, no less? Could this same man who had fabulous national political contacts which had brought monies and programs into their community; this same man who sat in the stands with them, cheering for their home teams and kids, have become so lust obsessed over some shameless, craven harlot? It seemed inconceivable!

And not even for any redemptive purpose; not to start a new life with her; not even to seek for himself, a different sort of life with that woman? No! But simply to get more money to buy more time with that immoral fille de joie? Just how sordid was their affair, really; exactly? How could any woman possibly hold such power over a man? What spells did her infamous family wrecking cunt cast upon Peterson? It was too disgustingly repulsive to imagine! The judge couldn't allow his mind to go there; afraid it might linger there too long; allured and fascinated by the iniquitous Ms. Sweets. Seedy, despicable weren't the right words for Her's and Peterson's unholy, tangled relationship. Macabre wasn't even the right word. This was vile; putrid, depraved; heinous beyond ungodly or something even worse. And, here it was, landed in his courtroom.

The judge shook his head in disbelief. He had no taste for this. He wanted no part in it. But duty called him. He knew he soon had to don his robe, leave his chambers, and go to his bench. But he didn't want to go. He felt the weight of the world on his shoulders:

'How did I draw the short straw to take this case? Why me?'

Ah, but he reminded himself that this sort of landmark case was exactly what he wanted to be part of, ever since he first entered law school. And now, after all his schooling and all his experiences, here it was. And he was its judge.

'How many times have I lifted my glass to toast Peterson's many accomplishments?'

The judge swallowed hard and wondered:

'How many fund raisers for worthy causes has Pete chaired? The new community ballpark on land donated by Peterson was Peterson Park. The huge payroll from Peterson's company kept this community viable. Hell, without Pete, there'd be no community. It would return to the weeds from which it had been hewn.

'Many in this courtroom owe their livelihoods to Peterson. Now a lot of these people want to see him get the death needle. I feel their blood lust. It hangs in the air above their low murmurs. People! But all that aside, I must proceed carefully here. I can't have a hung jury. I can't give his defense counsel grounds for a mistrial. I must take my time; confer with my clerks on motions before my rulings. I must

retreat to my chambers if I need time to research and think about the implications of my findings and my rulings. I must remember to pause; take my time; take recess breaks. I must be certain to check the statutes and the rulings of the higher courts. I must make sure I rule correctly. I must get it right the first time. Get it right the first time. Get it right the first time,' he repeatedly reminded himself.

Through this whole ordeal the assembly line at Peterson's factory had continued running as if there was nothing to worry about. Everyone had first believed it was just a coincidence that Pete couldn't be found. Perhaps Pete had a reaction to extreme grief? The man harbored a private side; guarded his business secrets. Hell, lots of men were like that. But Pete was dependable. He was always there for his wife and kids. No one could reconcile Pete's apprehension two hundred miles from town with the Pete they believed they knew. But then news of the photos leaked out. What was Pete doing with a porn star? And she was not just any porn star. She had a tawdry, wanton past. She'd broken up the marriages of a famous athlete and a revered movie star who previously had a squeaky-clean wholesome family man image. She was the worst sort of notoriously immoral vamp; the kind of asocial, outcast woman who entrapped men and took them for what she could get out of them.

The police report said when they picked Peterson up, he mumbled incoherently. He wore torn, dirty clothes; smelled like he hadn't bathed in weeks. He'd been drinking; couldn't walk a straight line. He'd let a scraggly beard grow out and he hadn't had a haircut in months. From all appearances, Pete was no longer Pete! He looked like a common vagrant; stooped over, shuffling along with his thumb out, trying to hitch a ride West.

The judge grimaced. He shook his head slightly, but with resolve. He had his oath to uphold. He needed to be impartial, but he knew that would be hard. His thoughts recalled past bar-b-q's with Peterson and their families:

'He couldn't have done something this heinous, could he?'

But then, what explained Peterson's disappearance? When Pete was picked up, he told the police he had slept under bridges and inside drainage culverts. He had all his identifications on him; driver's license, veteran's ID card, and four credit cards with over two hundred thousand dollars in available credit among them. The police report said he didn't resist arrest or try to flee.

'But why, Pete? Why in the world were you two hundred miles from home, disguised as a bum? Why didn't you stay in town and let the police interrogate you?'

After consultation with his attorney, Pete professed he was innocent. He had insisted on talking with a lawyer. After discussing his case with Defense counsel, Ms. Marcy Adams, he had refused to consider a plea deal. There would be no twenty to life sentence; no easy way for the judicial system to wash away this case. Now, all the preliminaries were over. Everything came down to this trial; in this courtroom; this one time roll of the dice. For Peterson, it would be acquittal or death. For the judge, the moment seemed incomprehensible; something akin to the preliminaries and the washing of his hands, before passing sentence for the crucifixion of the Christ.

Coglin, the District Attorney, had a very strong circumstantial case. He was one of those iron-willed zealous types; not the kind of man who compromised easily or handed out lenient pleas. There was an uncomfortable hint of sinister cruelty about Coglin's demeaner. People naturally disliked him; and for good reason. He was a powerful man and a dangerous man. And he knew it. He liked the image he had cultivated. He was a no nonsense, dogged, get his man, and hang him high, law and order, son of a bitch DA. Yesterday, Coglin reminded the judge of a vicious Doberman while at the preliminary hearing, he explained how he intended to prosecute the case. Coglin had snarled and salivated while placing the gory exhibit pictures under the judge's nose, The judge had to agree with Coglin. The pictures would be admitted as evidence.

'I can read Coglin's mind. He wants this one badly. He thinks Pete's conviction is his ticket to the governor's mansion.'

And Coglin made no bones about his goal. He told the TV cameras that the State of Florida was seeking the death penalty. But Coglin wanted something more than death. He wanted a public spectacle. He wanted the court to grant him free license to chew Peterson's head off. Like a vicious canine gnawing his guarded bone, Coglin would bark accusation after accusation at Peterson between his snarls. The judge could foresee the District Attorney's case presentation.

'He'll hurl inuendo after inuendo; spew hearsay after hearsay; titillate and infuriate; abruptly cut off witnesses' testimony, until he gets what he wants into the court record.'

Meanwhile, the demure Defense counsel, Marcy Adams, would rise and repeatedly object in her soft, seductive voice and her ice-cold composed demeanor.

'Coglin will want those objections overruled. He'll expect me to give him free reign to cut into Peterson. He'll want to fluster Peterson; make him angry; make him show a temper; make him confess his depraved moral weakness for the profligate porn star whore. Coglin would trick and trap Peterson into revealing himself as a duplicitous monster, wearing his family man image as a mere disguise; then, ultimately, as a pathetic lovelorn loser. And at the end of the trial, he'll want the jury to hand him Peterson's head on a pike; his bloody body's skin peeled off, stretched, and mounted; suitable for tacking onto an office wall in his new residence, the Governor's mansion.'

The District Attorney's evidence included salacious pictures of Pete with the porn star. They were damming photos. Pete was kissing her while his hands roamed all over her body. And, clearly, she was enjoying it. But the photos were still only circumstantial evidence.

Pete's attorney was a young rookie. She worked for a small law firm and had only two years' experience from working in the public defender's office. This was her first capital murder case. In chambers, she had seemed cool and collected enough. She carried herself well; great posture; confident; all business and unyielding; not the kind of lawyer who tried to smooth things over to get along. The judge couldn't help noticing her legs. Defense counsel Marcy Adams had exceptional legs. She had a winsome face, too:

'I'd love to take her for a tumble. Too bad I need to stay impartial.'

The judge knew the trial would be vicious; nasty. He took a deep breath, cleared his throat, and stepped through the door. It was showtime!

"All rise!" boomed the voice of the court bailiff. *"District Court is now in session. All ye who have business before this court, come ye now forward and present yourselves and your pleadings before the honorable judge Robert Strauss, now herein presiding."*

Standing now, John, the first businessman turned to his friend and whispered:

"Do you think Pete did it?"

Frank: "Hell no! He didn't do it. I know it looks bad for him, but I know Pete. He was always a good family man. I don't believe for one minute that he did it. He and Marge were always so much in love. I remember how Pete was head over heels crazy over Marge in high school. And he did everything for those kids; doted on them; tried to give them every advantage in life. He loved his kids. These murders are so out of character for him. He and Marge never fought. Every time I saw them together, I always saw love in their eyes. I'm telling you; I know Pete. There has to be some other explanation. It could not have been him. The cops have the wrong man."

"Please be seated," spoke the judge while seating himself in his big leather chair behind the bench. *"Mr. District Attorney, what do we have here?"*

"Docket number 25CM2653, State of Florida verses Peterson, your honor. The State of Florida seeks conviction for four counts of capital murder in the first degree."

"Very well. You may give your opening statement to the jury."

"Thank you, your honor," Coglin turned to the jury. *"Ladies and gentlemen, this is an aggravated homicide case. There were four vicious, heinous murders. The State of Florida will prove, beyond any reasonable doubt, that the defendant, Pete Peterson, acted with premeditation, meaning that he planned these murders; that he viciously and mercilessly carried them out; and that he sought to escape responsibility for his acts by attempting to flee Florida. The state will further show that the defendant had motive for committing these heinous crimes. The defendant carried on a secret love affair with a notorious porn star, a Ms. Sweets. The defendant's obsession with Ms. Sweets drove him to commit these murders in the hopes that he could cavort freely with Ms. Sweets and have more time with her.*

"The state will produce love letters that the defendant wrote to Ms. Sweets. In those letters, the defendant wrote not once, but no fewer than five times over several months before he murdered his wife and children, that he wanted to kill his wife and children; that he wanted to get rid of them from his life so he could spend more time in the arms of the wanton and shameless Ms. Sweets, and enjoy sinning with her more often in her bed. The defense will argue that these letters were merely expressions of desire; that the defendant never formed the requisite intent to murder his wife and children; that the defendant was not the real killer; that it was someone else; that there are questions surrounding the state's evidence; that the defendant tried to flee because he was frightened that you honest people would not give him a fair trial.

The defense will even throw out a few names of other people whom they say had motive, opportunity and means to do this dastardly deed. But, at the end of this trial, ladies and gentlemen, there will be no reasonable doubt that defendant Peterson's wife and children were murdered and that defendant Peterson committed those murders and that he alone must bear the full responsibility for what he did. And for murders this profoundly evil and heinous, there can be no less a burden of responsibility than death. We, as a civilized society, cannot carry the burden of having such a calloused, evil, sinful man as defendant Peterson living amongst us, even if he were to be incarcerated for life.

"Ladies and gentlemen, life behind bars is insufficient punishment for these horrific crimes. The state seeks to impose the exception rule for maximum capital punishment in this case. Defendant Peterson must not be allowed to live. The State of Florida seeks the death penalty for Defendant Peterson." The eyebrows of several jurors lifted. A few bit their lips. Suddenly, a terrifying reality made its presence known. A man's life was being delivered into their hands. Many jurors looked at Peterson through eyes which bespoke his reality:

'We have been empowered to kill you.'

A hushed murmur settled over the attendees in the courtroom gallery.

"Defense counsel, please present your opening statement."

"Thank you, your honor." Demure Marcy Adams, defense counsel, rose slowly and confidently from the defendant's table. With measured steps she walked to the jury box while smiling warmly to the jurors; making eye contact with every juror.

"Ladies and gentlemen, defendant Peterson is an innocent man. He told me he didn't do it and I believe him. The prosecution would have you rush to judgment in this case. The evidence you will hear from Mr. Coglin is purely circumstantial. He has no witness to

these murders. Any one of more than a thousand people could have committed them. He will read love letters to you. Many people get emotional over their love affairs. That's not at all unusual. Many people feel passionate about their love interests; many people write love letters while they are in their fits of passion; and many will even say that they love someone so much that they would kill for them. But that doesn't mean they would actually do that.

"Ladies and gentlemen, there's a tiny gland in our brains called the amygdala. When it becomes excited by a strong emotion, like erotic love, it will sometimes cause us to temporarily take leave of our senses. That's called the limbic effect. That happens while the brain becomes controlled by its amygdala produced hormones, and while those hormones cause some people to temporarily behave under the control of their limbic effect, they may act emotionally. But notice that I used the word temporarily. That's because the limbic effect is temporary.

"The defense will produce an expert witness that will explain this temporary effect in more detail to you. The expert will explain that, while the defendant did write those letters, they could not possibly have had a permanent effect upon his actions. In truth, my innocent client, Mr. Peterson, had no more inclination to murder the victims than any of you had. Shortly after he wrote those letters, Mr. Peterson's emotional passions subsided, because the limbic effect is never permanent. Other hormones reassert their control over the brain and the mind's limbic passions subside.

"Considerable time passed between the writing of those letters and the murders. It's simply not possible that the defendant could have sustained such a high level of passion for Ms. Sweets for such a lengthy time. Thus, the prosecution's motive for these murders is not credible. Besides lack of motive, the rest of the prosecution's case has fatal flaws. They have no weapon. They have no witness. After you hear the prosecution's lurid, fantastical tales of a sordid love affair,

you will be left with only one reasonable conclusion. And that is this: The State is unable to prove beyond a reasonable doubt that our defendant, our dear, good-natured Pete Peterson, committed these murders. In truth, none of us know who committed these murders. The District Attorney certainly doesn't know. All he has to offer you is his imaginary, salacious fabrication of events; but he cannot give you solid, irrefutable proof that anything he imagines to be true is actually true. You must honor what your reasonable doubt demands you to do. You cannot convict an innocent man. The consequences of an erroneous conviction are simply too great. You must acquit Pete Peterson." As Marcy Adams walked back to the defendant's table, several jurors were seen nodding their heads.

John:	*"Have you seen the girl?"* The first businessman whispered, leaning into the second businessman.
Frank:	*"No, I don't know anything about her, other than what I've heard on the news or read in the paper. Do you know her? Is she from around here?"*
John:	*"Oh, Frank, you've got to have a look at her! You've got to look at some of her films."*
Frank:	*"Films? Joyce told Mandy she worked in some night club. She's an actress?"*
John:	*"Sweet Jesus, Frank! What rock do you live under? She's Ms. Sweets, the hottest, newest porn star. She's won all sorts of porn awards for most erotic actress; best seduction scene; best classic porn; best threesome performer; most authentic orgasm scene. She's amazing. You need to watch some of her films. Then you'll see why the prosecution case is credible. The woman is a porn sensation. She loves her erotic acting roles. She's a real tease; but so much more than a tease. She loves to fuck. It comes through on the screen. You have to see her. She laughs and giggles and*

chortles through every porn scene like she can't possibly get enough cock to satisfy her. She's highly seductive and incredibly emotive. She performs the most erotic porn I've ever seen."

Frank: *"Okay John, yes. I've heard of her. She made the papers a few weeks ago. Isn't she the same porn star who's getting married to old Sam Dolzmick?"*

John: *"Yes. That's the one. He's crazy over her. He's thrilled that she'll have him. He even published their prenup. Imagine an eighty-year-old man paying a young wife $20 million a week just to have sex with him once a week."*

Frank: *"Well, maybe that's all his heart can handle."*

John: *"Probably true. But after she collects her first billion, he gives her another half of his estate when he dies, as long as she stays married to him for five more years or until his death, whichever comes first. That's the eight billion dollars deal she cut for herself. It's right there in the published prenup. On top of that, Sam is financing eighteen full feature length porn films. He wants her to star in them."*

Frank: *"Wait. How about Sam's kids? What do they think of the prenup?"*

John: *"Four kids. They get to split his remaining eight billion four ways."*

Frank: *"Wow! Good to be in the lucky sperm club. Well, what about the films? Why eighteen?"*

John: *"They're based on a book series called 'The Secret Butterfly Series™.' Sam listens to audio books. He digs erotica; loves listening to porn stars expressing themselves while they orgasm; loves hearing them talking about how they are getting wet and coming while they orgasm; loves hearing their bantering with their porn partners about how they feel while they are getting penetrated and the things they talk about while they are fucking. He claims pornography is the future of film; claims we left the family friendly 'Hayes Standard' for the motion picture industry's present standard 'R' rated world long ago, back when social morality first began to disintegrate. Sam says we are now about to take another huge societal leap forward into secular immorality."*

Frank: *"You mean into an abyss of sin and debauchery?"*

John: *"Yes, exactly. Sam opines that society is salivating to embrace X rated films. X films, according to Sam, are about to become the new social mainstream norm. Sam spends five to ten hours every day watching porn or listening to X rated audio tapes. That's how he came to his fascination with Ms. Sweets, this porn star woman. She is doing the voice recordings for the audio books of the Series."*

Frank: *"How so?"*

John: *"Because Sam knows the author of the Series. It's his cousin. She goes by her 'Rosemary Ness Bitner' pen name. So, Sam naturally bought the audio tapes of her first few books and listened to them. That's how he found out the narrator's voice belonged to Ms. Sweets. He arranged for his cousin to introduce him to her. I happen to know Sam's cousin."*

Frank: *"Really? What's she like?"*

John: *"She's old, like Sam. I'd put her in her late seventies. She's the most secretive person you'll ever know; lives in a cabin in remote British Columbia; loves seclusion. She comes to Florida to visit Sam and friends, mostly during the winter months to get away from the deep snows of BC. Anyway, she and I, through Sam, became friends. She doesn't mince words. She told me that Ms. Sweets gave old Sam the greatest fuck he'd ever had in is life. And Sam knows he hasn't got much more time. So, he's decided to marry her."*

Frank: *"Okay, well, it's his money. But how does Pete fit into this? I mean, if Ms. Sweets is going to marry Sam, why was she seeing Pete?"*

John: *"Do I need to spell it out for you, Frank?"*

Frank: *"I don't get it."*

John: *"Her affair with Pete started before she met Sam. She's the prosecution's motive for the murders, Frank. The prosecution is alleging that Pete got it on with Ms. Sweets. They have pictures of the two of them having dinner together; kissing; warm embraces; you know, lovers' type stuff. They also have credit card receipts where Pete was paying Ms. Sweets $50,000 for a weekend with her and pictures of the two of them on Pete's boat."*

Frank: *"Let me guess. She was wearing a bikini?"*

John: *"Close. Sometimes she wore a bikini. Other times she was naked."*

Frank: *"Oh. So, Pete strayed a little. It happens. But that doesn't make him a murderer."*

John: *"No? Well, try this. He borrowed a million on his business. And the business credit line shows he paid sweet Ms. Sweets, porn star, over a million in the past year. He was giving that porn star everything he had. The only way he could afford to keep seeing her was to murder his wife and get her insurance and her family trust's assets. That got him another twelve million. And lots more time with Ms. Sweets."*

Frank: *"Sounds like Pete went crazy."*

John: *"Joyce thinks that's what happened. She believes the porn star fogged Pete's brain; made him insane with lust over her. And you know how strong Pete is. Joyce thinks Marge may have tried to confront him or get in his way somehow. And Pete just snapped."*

Frank: *"Maybe. But the kids? Why would he kill his own kids?"*

John: *"That's the part that doesn't fit. The prosecution argues that one of them saw their mother's murder. But the defense is saying that they were all away from the house when Marge's murder happened. That's where the prosecution's evidence gets shaky. It's the possible flaw in the prosecution's case. But no one knows where the kids were. All anyone knows is that they were murdered later, about eight hours after Marge was murdered."*

Frank: *"You know so much."*

John: *"I've read everything I could find on it."*

Frank: *"This porn star. Tell me about her. What's the big attraction about her?"*

John: *"Everything. She's gorgeous; but it's so much more than her breathtaking beauty. It's the way she handles herself while she's making her porn films. It's how she carries her body, the way she smiles and moves her facial muscles, her expressiveness; how she caresses a man's face and head and shoulders and arms with her hands; her way of seductively touching a man; and her confidence about who she is. She loves the seduction art. She loves performing her porn. She does it for the joy of it. She's caring and loving in the ways she romances a man's cock. I mean she's so damn seductive and so glorious and casually free about doing what she does, you cannot help falling in love with her.*

"In one interview she did, she talked about how seeing a partner's cock for the first time makes her blood flame hot; makes her clit start swelling up and her vaginal

channel get slippery wet. She said she feels the same free-dom a butterfly feels when she starts taking her partner's cock in her hands and begins licking it. She doesn't give any thought to anything other than totally enjoying her love making with that cock. All her other thoughts simply fall away.

"When you watch her performing, you get the feeling that she loves being immoral; like immorality is her reli-gion and she's the high priestess of sin; and proud of it; very confident and proud that her shameless promiscuity is the correct religion for all mankind. You can tell she loves her own body and how pleased she is while plying her eroticism. You can read her mind while she performs. You can tell she's understanding that millions of men will be watching the film. She loves that. She loves fucking for the cameras. She makes your mouth water. You'll see. She makes you want to submit to her; give her anything she wants; give her everything you have. You'll want to kiss her; hug her; hold her; worship her. You'll want to fuck her so badly that you'd be willing to die from exhaustion from fucking her."

Frank: *"She's that hot?"*

John: *"No; hotter. You'll see what I mean when you look at her porn pictures."*

Frank: *"The pictures the DA will be showing the jury?"*

John: *"Yes. You can see them for yourself. They're online. You'll notice how her expression lights up when her lips begin kissing the head of a penis, and while she's licking the shaft of a penis, and when a penis first touches her lady lips to begin its penetration. She's absolutely enthralled to be performing those intimate poses. She titillates and excites males' amygdales, causing their limbic minds to flood with lust and adoration for her. She leaves you speechless; breathless; pining for her; consumed with overwhelming desires to love her and fuck her."*

Frank: *"And the DA believes her salacious porn pictures will enrage the jury, right?"*

John: *"Yes. I'm certain he believes Ms. Sweet's porn pictures will inflame and outrage the jurors. He thinks pictures of Ms. Sweets joyously performing fellatio and beaming her victoriously gleeful smiles while streams of semen from male penises spurt onto her tongue will thoroughly disgust the jurors; make them feel revulsion; incense them that Pete could ever contemplate murdering his family to have more time with such a brazen whore. Those pictures show Ms. Sweets to be a million times more sensuous and more casual about her immorality than I could ever describe her antics in words."*

Frank: *"That's what makes the DA's motive argument so compelling, right?"*

John: *"Yes; but it's hard to know if his strategy will work."*

Frank: *"What do you mean? The DA has the gory murder pictures. He has those pictures of Ms. Sweets performing disgusting immoral acts. He has Pete's love letters. And he has Pete trying to shed his identity and flee the state. Why wouldn't his strategy work?"*

John: *"Marcy Adams."*

Frank: *"Pete's defense lawyer? What does she have to do with it? All she has is some goof ball shrink who will say the amygdala's hormone effect is temporary."*

John: *"I know; but did you get a good look at her?"*

Frank: *"Yes, she's gorgeous, why?"*

John: *"Well, did you notice how several of the male jurors looked at her while she sat at the Defendant's table; and how their eyes stayed riveted on her while she gave her opening statement?"*

Frank: *"I didn't pay attention to them. I was focused on her."*

John: *"My point, exactly."*

Frank: *"Huh?"*

John: *"While you looked at her, what were you thinking?"*

Frank: *"Of undressing her; of kissing her; possibly, hopefully fucking her."*

John: *"That's my point. Don't you think several of the male jurors had the same thoughts?"*

Frank: *"Oh. Yeah, I suppose so. She's beautiful, and the way she carries herself and how her voice sounds are both very sexy."*

John: *"That's why I think the DA's strategy of using Ms. Sweet's porn pictures could backfire."*

Frank: *"Huh?"*

John: *"Well, think about it. If those porn pictures excite the amygdale of male jurors; and if that tiny gland's hormones takes limbic control of their minds, wouldn't it then follow that their limbic lusts might vicariously transfer those lusts to Marcy Adams? Wouldn't those lusts make them want to please Marcy Adams by bringing a verdict of not guilty?"*

Frank: *"Oh, I don't think so. Jurors are instructed to follow the evidence."*

John: *"Yes, their rational minds are supposed to follow the evidence. But I think Marcy Adams is playing a more subtle game than the DA is playing. She seems to know that minds sometimes decide based upon their limbic yearnings. You noticed how her nipples strained against her silk blouse; how her breasts peeked out from beneath her suit jacket?"*

Frank: "Yes."

John: "And you noticed her pelvic concavity and the tightness of her suit skirt?"

Frank: "Hard not to notice."

John: "Did you catch the way she stood before that one juror, the handsome young man with the curly blond hair?"

Frank: "You mean how she kind of lingered in front of him?"

John: "Yes, but also how she shifted her weight from one foot to the other; and while she did that, she gave her pelvis a slight upward, forward lift? I don't think very many people noticed that. It was very subtle; but I think she was signaling that young juror that she wanted to fuck him."

Frank: "That would be illegal. Are you sure?"

John: "No, I'm not sure. But watching the two of them, it seemed to me that they knew each other somehow."

Frank: "The jurors took oaths. The judge questioned them about that. They all represented that they had no conflicts."

John: "Yeah, I know. But did you catch her 'come hither,' coquettish smile while she slowly nodded her head, suggesting that the jurors should agree with her?"

Frank: "Yes. It was hard not to notice. She makes me salivate."

John: "Me, too. When she walked back to the defense table, I watched the eyes of a few male jurors. Their eyes were riveted on her tush. I'm sure they imagined removing her skirt, peeling off her panties and fucking her. Their minds were not thinking rationally. Let your own imagination run free for a moment. Could you see Marcy Adams performing as a porn star?"

Frank: "I suppose so. Yeah, I could see that. What are you suggesting?"

John: "I'm just saying: It's not hard to imagine that some of those male jurors imagined her doing just that. I think *she had those jurors imagining she was lavishing all sorts of erotic splendor upon their penises; driving them crazy out of their minds with lust for her."*

Frank: *"So, you're saying the evidence is irrelevant; that it doesn't matter whether Pete murdered his family or not? You're saying the only thing that matters is whom the jury wants to win; DA Coglin, or Marcy Adams? And you think she has preconditioned some of the jury males to fantasize they'll get to fuck her if she wins the case?"*

John: *"Yes, that's what I'm saying. Trials are a funny thing; especially a murder trial. Sometimes they come down to whom the jury wants to win; the DA or the defense counsel. It doesn't matter why they want one side or the other to win. The only thing that matters is the verdict. The facts, the evidence, and the logic don't always matter. If some of those jurors want Marcy Adams to win, for whatever reason they hold in their minds, they'll find an excuse for the DA to lose. The DA has no murder weapon. The murders were all done with a knife. The police haven't found it."*

Frank: *"So some jurors' vicarious dreams of fucking Marcy Adams or watching her perform as a porn star might prevail over justice for Pete's wife and kids?"*

John: *"Might. Just saying it's possible. I watched her and the way the jurors responded to her. I believe my eyes."*

Frank: *"I can't imagine Pete stabbing his kids."*

John: *"Me neither. But evidence or lack of evidence is irrelevant. Obviously, Pete wanted to ditch his family for Ms. Sweets. The letters and the photos make Pete look terrible. But how does the DA explain no murder knife and no witness? Pete can't account for his whereabouts when the murders supposedly took place. Pete can't explain why he looked like a shiftless vagrant when the police nabbed him. The DA has a strong circumstantial case. But the DA can't place Pete at the crime when the murders took place. So, just saying, with this jury and Marcy Adams as his lawyer, Pete's got a chance."*

Frank: *"Where does Pete say he was?"*

John: *"With Ms. Sweets. But she waffled about corroborating his alibi."*

Frank: *"Why?"*

John: *"Not sure."*

A middle-aged woman was seated in the row in front of the talkative businessmen. She turned around to address the source of her annoyance:

"Gentlemen, I am trying to understand why my dear sister and darling nephews and niece were murdered. This horror is difficult enough without having to listen to the two of you raving about the glorious immorality of some disgusting porn star. Please respect my distress. If you must extol the prurient qualities of Ms. Sweets, please have the decency to remove yourselves from the courtroom. Why don't you both just leave?" Her request was more of a demand, conveyed with an angry, hostile look.

John: *"You know, Frank, she's got a good idea. This is a waste of time anyway. The lawyers will be at the bench or in chambers, arguing rules of evidence and formalities the rest of today and probably a lot of tomorrow. Look, let's go to my place. Today is Mandy's bridge day. She won't be home until five PM or later. I've got something you should see."*

A half hour later, Frank and John were seated in John's home theater room, watching a porn film starring Ms. Sweets, performing on a full theater sized screen.

John: *"Can you now see what I was telling you? Are you sensing the underlying vibes of glorious, triumphant, moral degeneracy and natural, casual freedom that seems to ooze from every pore of her body? Can't you just feel it? I know I can. It flows from her body language and radiates from her smiling face. She's delighted to be creating her gorgeous pornography. She loves performing. She's a virtuoso; a perfectionist artisan. I can't help myself. I adore her; can't get enough of her. And that chortling voice she has! So mirthful, so pleasing to be promiscuous and shameless about it. Her voice penetrates me, right into the depths of my soul. I lust after her. Are you feeling what I'm feeling?"*

Frank: *"Yes, I think so. It's like a different part of my mind governs my feelings now. It's kind of the opposite of the feelings I have when I'm in church."*

John: *"Yes, exactly. Your limbic mind is governing you, not your logical, cortex controlling mind. It's like in church you are meant to feel submissive and docile and obedient. But with the limbic effect of porn, you feel released and free und uninhibited. This must be what God tried to prevent us from feeling when he told Adam and Eve to not eat from the tree of knowledge. He did not want us to feel this way."*

Frank: *"Why not?"*

John: *"Because, well, hell Frank, look at her. Think about how you feel. That must be how the Gods themselves feel. It's like when you let go of all the do's and don'ts that religions hammer into you and you allow your limbic system to release you. You feel uninhibited, free, and joyous; like there's no such thing as sin; like there's nothing to feel guilty about. You feel like you have become God, yourself. You just want to go to her and make love with her, don't you?"*

Frank: *"Yes, You're right. It's true. Absolutely, I do."*

John: *"Well, the way we feel now must be how Pete felt about her. I know it's how old Sam feels about her. He told me he felt that he had to have her when he saw her one film where she's kissing some man while he's fingering her; and she's thrusting her vagina into his fingers, loving how he's heating her up and getting her wet.*

"Sam said watching her thrusting like that was like putting a hot blowtorch under his limbic zone. She ignited passions in him that he'd never felt before. He told me every fiber of his being came alive. He said he felt like a teenager again. He believed if only he could perform cunnilingus with her; have her clitoris know his tongue; and if only he could fuck her and ejaculate into her glorious pussy, he'd feel vindicated and reborn as a man. He'd feel validation for being blessed with a long life. That's what made Sam determine that this young porn goddess was his life's calling. He believes she was placed there, before him, to extend his life; and for him to discover her and mentor her and advance her station in life."

Frank: *"That's crazy. Sam's just cunt obsessed. He's always been cunt obsessed."*

John: *"Yes. That's true about Sam. He told me, ever since he saw that scene, all he could think about was holding her, kissing her, and fucking her. That's what made him decide he needed to marry her; give her half his wealth."*

Frank: *"At his age?"*

John: *"Yes, age doesn't matter in a decision like that for a man like Sam. He feels life starting to slip away. It's about holding onto happiness for the rest of his remaining life. And Ms. Sweets makes him happy. Look at the film. Do you get the vibe how she conveys her message of righteous immorality; her indignity over societal norms? When she performs her mouthwatering seductions, exquisite fellatios, and fornications can you feel her inner confidence?*

"She projects the rightness of her immorality; like it's sanctified. Can't you feel it? Doesn't her persona seem to proclaim that her immorally is acceptable and justified and right in an absolute sense of what is humanly right? Can't you see that no religious principles could ever dissuade her from her porn craft or distract her focus from creating the world's most sensational porn? Are you sharing my feelings here? Can you intuit that Ms. Sweets has positioned herself as the ultimate deviation from traditional moral principals? Can you sense that she is supremely confident, very poised about her sexuality; very secure in her stunning beauty?"

Frank: *"Yes, yes; a thousand times yes. I do see that about her. I see and feel everything you see and feel. I agree. She is exceptional; even beyond exceptional. I'm not as big of a porn aficionado as you or Sam, but I have seen quite a bit of it. I admit, I've never seen any porn star as beautiful, as seductive, as poised, or confident as this Ms. Sweets. I've looked at porn from many of the top hundred rated porn stars. None of them can hold a candle to her. You can see an inner luminance radiating from her face and skin. She's an angelic presence amongst us, as if she's arrived from eternity to lead us mere mortals into a more perfect world. Obviously, she loves what she does. Obviously, she's the ultimate dream woman; the most beautiful, most erotically titillating and most creative of all porn stars. I believe that now, and in the hundred years before her and in the hundred years that will come after her, no other woman will surpass her feminine attributes.*

"I admit she is stunning and she seems very natural and completely at ease while performing her porn. But doesn't Sam, at his age, find her behavior base and slutty, like all the other porn stars? And, after seeing her performing in hundreds of scenes, kissing other men's penises while they spurt semen cum onto her tongue, how does he cope with that?"

John: *"He doesn't think of her performances as base or slutty. He sees her as Asherah, the pagan goddess of the Hebrew tribes before Abraham and Sara; before the Hebes discovered God."*

Frank: *"Asherah was a goddess?"*

John: *"Yes. She was the fertility goddess. She assured the continuation of the tribe. They had ritual services. For a man to be worthy of tribal membership he needed to commit himself to the perpetuation of the tribe. He needed to cleanse himself in a ritual bath; then copulate with the temple prostitute who represented Asherah. He needed to enter her vagina with his penis and ejaculate semen into her; share sacred human communion with her inside her holy of holies. He needed to be circumcised before he was allowed to enter her, to be certain that he was making a clean offering. The ceremonial services included animal sacrifices and feasting.*

"The ritual fornications opened their limbic minds to the glory of humanity and the perpetuation of the tribe.

This mind set fortified the tribal members' belief that their loyalties were to the tribe and its expansion. They felt it was their righteous duty to conquer others' lands and plunder their wealth; and to tithe ten percent of their takings to the temple prostitutes. The men even carried wooden carvings of Asherah, her open vagina prominently featured, with them into battle. I think that's where the idea of having 'a woman to die for' came into being. These ancient warriors were committed to furthering the glory and wealth of their prostitutes. They performed their ritual fornication services before they departed on hunts and war parties. They also performed their fornications at special commemorative times; when they atoned for their individual transgressions against other tribal members, and when they celebrated their status as a unified, free people."

Frank: *"So Sam thinks Ms. Sweets is a living reincarnation of Asherah? He thinks her pornography is a throwback to the times when her fornications were sacred, holy rites?"*

John: *"Yes, absolutely. He believes ancient prostitution worship has never died; rather, it has continued, secretly underground and hidden away for thousands of years. Sam believes that human males have always secretly adored prostitutes and whores. Men who secretly keep porn magazines and digital libraries of porn are simply continuing the ancient practice of keeping sculpted idols of Asherah in their possession. Asherah has been transformed into our modern-day porn goddesses. Humans once prayed to Asherah. They glorified her vagina. Ancient carvings of her prominently featured her vagina. Her procreative power was worshipped. Men prayed to her and they died in their hunts and battles in their honor of her. Males' limbic minds needed the psychological assurance that Asherah's fabulous cunt was reliably with them; appreciating their manhood; accepting them in union with her; reassuring them of their virility and worthiness. Today's minds have those same needs. That's why pin up girls are painted on airplanes and weapons of war in our modern times. That's why society is beginning to worship its porn stars. The limbic human mind has not changed. It still needs a 'femme superior' goddess to reassure it of its worthiness.*

Sam believes today's porn stars and prostitutes uniquely satisfy the male limbic mind's need for Asherah's reassuring presence. They are there; capable and willing to 'turn on' their passionate lovemaking for every passable man who tithes them. In modern terms, tithing of animals, jewels, and ivory has been replaced by money payments. In return for payment to his porn star, the male receives acceptance, confidence; and a sense of belonging to a select fraternity of devoted males who have also copulated with the prostitute. He becomes part of a group, a modern-day tribe, so to speak, who are committed to furthering the prostitute's wealth and fame. He also receives genuine intimate love from the prostitute; that vitally necessary human need to belong to and bond with another caring, understanding human.

"Sam regards prostitutes who are capable of 'turning on' their love making with several men in one day as exceptionally valuable humans, for their social function is vital for harmonious communal living. Porn stars are particularly valuable, in Sam's eyes, for they embody the essence of humanity's most fundamental need: the need to copulate and create. Sam prefers the company of

prostitutes and porn stars to the company of women he calls 'regular' or 'conventional' women. He claims porn stars and prostitutes are easier to understand, less complicated, less neurotic, and easier for him to relate to. He doesn't care for vague, uncertain, and illusive. He prefers unpretentious and forthright with unbridled talent. He compares women to horses, opining that prostitutes and porn stars are analogous to prized, untamed, race horses; whereas ordinary, conventional, domesticated women are more like simple trail horses. Sam prefers race horses. They challenge him; make his blood run hot.

"In Sam's eyes, Ms. Sweets is even more special than a prized race horse. She's a modern-day goddess, performing her eternal, sacred porn craft and displaying her extraordinary skill sets, lifting her high above all ordinary women and lesser porn stars."

Frank: *"Like the flying horse that took Mohammed to heaven, separating him from ordinary mortals?"*

John: *"Yeah, something like that; whatever. In Sam's mind, Ms. Sweets is the ultimate femme extraordinaire. He has this adoration thing for her. He knows she loves performing her scenes. He claims they are her ways of releasing her erotic soul to bond with her partners' souls through her holy pornography. It's all very unifying and humanistic. He knows all aspects of pornography make Ms. Sweets happy. He knows she thoroughly enjoys all variations of foreplay stimulation, fornication, and fellatio. And he's thrilled to help facilitate her happiness. He tells me to not get hung up on the morality question. He disparages moralizers as obsolete holdovers from Victorian times. He tells me to instead focus on Ms. Sweets' facial expressions; on how much she obviously loves what she's doing. He tells me to pay particular attention to her eyes because they are windows into her soul. He claims her eyes are happy, joyous eyes.*

"He believes her soul enters his through her eyes. When he makes love with her, he sees inner lust fires in her eyes. He swears her lust fires suck in a man's soul and consume it; burn away his morality; turn his religious learnings to ashes. Then she blows his religion away, replacing it with the man's reborn, immoral soul."

Frank: *"And she's cavalier about her soul snatchings?"*

John: *"Absolutely, she is. Ms. Sweets laughs and chortles while devouring a man's morality. She consumes righteousness. She relishes her soul-ravishing while her partner's semen flows freely and untroubled inside her; until his surrendered morality becomes a spent wisp of his former soul, either consumed within her vagina, or swallowed irretrievably down her ravenous sperm guzzling throat. And once she's captured a man's soul, she keeps it.*

"She completes her lovers' conversions by consorting with them many times afterwards. Their immorality is reinforced. They find leaving her and returning to their moral ways as impossible as fitting into outgrown clothes. Her sea of immorality engulfs and subsumes their impotent souls. Unable to resist her, they become addicted to her; forever captives to her charms and favors. And they truly love her, as Sam truly loves her; and as early tribesmen loved their goddess Asherah."

Frank: *"Those early tribes, those Asherah worshippers, seemed engaged in endless wars with other tribes. Is that where modern pornography is taking us?"*

John: *"Maybe. I don't know. There's a clash of cultures between those civilizations that want to adore women who flaunt their pussies and those civilizations that want women's pussies hidden away. Our civilization champions women; gives them equal rights. Some other civilizations view women as a threat to social order. And they deny women equal rights. This conflict tells us that the female pussy is the source of male emotions. Pussies drive men crazy."*

Frank: *"And Ms. Sweets excels at driving men crazy. Her website offers her fans hundreds of her porn films. How can Sam kiss her mouth and perform oral sex with her after watching her do all the things she does with so many other men's penises? How does he block those things from his mind?"*

John: *"Sam doesn't have guilt hang ups or trepidations about her porn craft. Sam avers that what happens inside her mouth and inside her vagina is more holy and life affirming than any death offering sacrifice which any priest has ever performed upon any altar. When he kisses her, he feels like he's honoring her glory as a woman. While he performs cunnilingus, he believes he's offering homage to her sacred fecundity. It's Sam's way of blessing her. It's the conditioning of his frame of mind. Repetition does that. It reinforces belief. The more profligate she is, the more Sam's adoration for her increases. In that sense, he's more than her enabler. He's her champion, facilitator, and love slave."*

Frank: *"John, wait! Hold it right there. Back the film up to where she undoes her bra from the front to reveal her boobs."*

John: *"Okay. ……. Here?"*

Frank: *"Yeah. I want to hear what she's saying there, one more time."*

John: *"Okay." John replayed the film tape.*

Frank: *"Did you catch that? She's talking to the guy's penis about billions of dollars of jewels? Then she's talking about taking his soul away. She talks like she knows something and wants to put it on film. Then she's kissing the guy and looking into his eyes. But, before that, she was talking to his dick; telling his dick it will be with her forever. I've never heard any woman say things like that. Could you make sense of that?"*

John: *"Yes. But that's because I've read the books of THE SECRET BUTTERFLY SERIES™. She's taking her lines from a scene in the Series. Sam says it's all true."*

CHAPTER TWO

BLOOD JEWELS

Frank: *"What? Sam's cousin Rosemary's Series; the part about the jewels?"*

John: *"Yes. You heard that right. Sam knew the real-life 'Marvin' character from the Series. Marvin set up the escape lines to get the Jews out of Hitler's Germany. He worked it so that he got paid in jewels. The Series explains in detail how Marvin did it. Sam knew the real-life woman who is the Series' 'Susan' character, too. Sam was one of her real-life lovers. Marvin got paid in jewels to get the Jews out. Later, when Germany started losing the war, Marvin set up rat lines to get the top Nazis out. He was fast friends with Argentina's Colonel Juan Peron. Marvin and Susan were scam artists. They hauled off over a hundred billion dollars' worth of diamonds, rubies, and emeralds in today's dollars. Marvin and Susan never even paid a dime of taxes on their huge take. It's all unreported. Sam knows where the jewels are. Susan was something else. A femme among femmes; a totally hot babe. Even though she was Marvin's woman, she was the love of Sam's life before he met Ms. Sweets. Susan was the consummate whore. She even did Juan Peron. Her partnership with*

Marvin, her wits, and her fabulous pussy made her the wealthiest woman in America. Ironic, isn't it? The Nazis did all that killing and plundering; and the lion's share of their loot ends up being owned by an American whore. Amazing how the world works!"

Frank: *"How does Sam know all this? How does he know where the jewels are?"*

John: *"He was the photographer for the explicit pictures of Susan' peccadillos. Marvin and Sam were close. Marvin loved watching Susan doing other men. The more she whored, the more Marvin loved her. He was obsessed with her. See, Marvin had all these pictures of Susan taken while she was doing their wealth management clients. Sam's real last name is Ep. He did what lots of Jews did after the war. He got his name changed. In the Series, cousin Rosemary used Sam's real name: Ep. He photographed Susan doing himself and Marvin on top of a mountain of the jewels. Ep was into filming and photography; one of the first to use a camera's time delay feature."*

Frank: *"Sounds crazy."*

John: *"Yeah, but it's true. Sam swears: It's all true. The jewels are real. They exist. Sam knows where they are."*

Frank: *"This Series is all fiction, right?"*

John: *"Yes, mostly. But that part about the jewels is true. The characters and story line are fictional. But the part about the jewels for Jews; and rat lines for jewels from escaping Nazis is real. The story about the jewels is real. I've seen the jewels with my own eyes. Sam showed me two huge mason jars filled with emeralds, rubies, and diamonds. And those were only a tiny fraction of what Marvin took from Nazi Germany."*

Frank: *"Sweet Jesus! Well, how is it that Ms. Sweets is talking about the jewels in this film? What does she know and how does she know it?"*

John: *"From Sam. He loves her. He has trouble keeping his mouth shut when he's in love. His penis gets the best of him. No doubt his limbic mind opened up to her."*

Frank: *"Well, what is the spiritual stuff she's saying to her porn partner and his penis?"*

John: *"That's what's got Sam so fired up. That's why he's going to marry her."*

Frank: *"I've never heard any woman say things like that; lavishing praise upon a penis like that. It's adoration; more like worship. It kind of sucks you in and takes your mind into hers. It doesn't let go of you. I feel captured by her; like I'd do anything for her."*

CHAPTER THREE

BUTTERFLY DNA

John:	"Sam's cousin, Rosemary, says that's her DNA thing. It's got its hook into you. You might as well face it. You're at the beginning of the seduction process. That spiritual stuff Ms. Sweets is saying is real. Cousin Rosemary researched it. She talked to this old shrink, Mrs. O'Dell, about it. This Mrs. O'Dell knew the woman who is the actual 'Marty' character in the Series. Marty was Susan's actual daughter in real life. They both understood the spiritual powers of their Pagan DNA. They called it their 'Butterfly DNA.' It captures a man's limbic mind; makes him powerless to resist the woman's seductions. It's a power aphrodisiac for the women who have it. It makes some women turn nymphomaniac; they become totally uninhibited fuck bunnies. Marty, the key heroine from Rosemary's Series, said her butterfly DNA made her want to 'flutter,' which was her code way of saying she wanted to fuck. Marty swore she experienced a spiritual butterfly transformation. She lived it. She explained it to Sam's cousin, Rosemary, how it takes place in a woman."
Frank:	"Like she became a butterfly? Sounds crazy."
John:	"No. It is not crazy. It's true. It's how butterfly spirits interact with human spirits between humans' reincarnations.

Human spirits transform into butterflies' spirits; and butterfly spirits reenter human spirits in humans' new lives. The butterfly spirit loves freedom. It must have it. It wants out of its cocoon. It's a powerful driver. It's what makes humans human. Rosemary met another woman named Sheila, who also experienced it. She described her spiritual transformation in Rosemary's book: LUST WHEELS©. Her transformation took place when she met the spirit of Marty at the butterflies' secret spiritual place called the 'Lust Wheel.'"

Frank: *"And Sam believes this stuff?"*

John: *"He does. He says it's easier than believing in God. He thinks it makes more sense."*

Frank: *"And this phenomenon causes women to become promiscuous? Turns many of them into nymphomaniacs?"*

John: *"Yes, Frank, absolutely! Look around you. Look at all the women who are getting into porn. Porn is freeing them. This is not some passing fad. You are witnessing our societal transformation."*

Frank: *"True. Okay, I'll bite. So, tell me more about Sam's cousin, Rosemary. What do you know about her?"*

John: *"You should bite. I'm telling you; I saw the jewels she wrote about. Everything I'm telling you is real. And the nympho DNA thing and the butterfly spirit thing are believably real, too; more believable than religious homilies.*

"As far as his cousin, Rosemary: I only know what Sam told me about her. She was from the poor cousins' branch of Sam's family. She was born in some Appalachian mountain hollow, in a shack of a house beside a creek, some place in West Virginia or Kentucky. It was at the end of a dead-end dirt road into a hidden God forsaken pit called Skunks' Hollow. The family lived in a

clapboard wood and cardboard shack. No electricity, no plumbing. Her mother and sisters died of Spanish Flu. Her father didn't want her. He gave her to be raised by a neighboring family.

"That family who took her in were dirt poor Hill Billy people; totally uncivilized; missing teeth, unintelligible speech, unwashed, unkept, ragged moth-eaten clothes when they bothered to cover themselves. A wretched place for a young girl. They had three boys. When Rosemary was given to them, she was three or four. The adults made Rosemary work chores from the time she got there. She had to sweep the floors from her first day there. She remembers learning how to milk their cow when she was about six or seven. She was responsible for filling the coal bin and shoveling coal into the stove that heated the shack. And she had to rake the furnace's ashes, shovel them into a bucket, careful not to burn herself; and carry them to an open dump, about twenty yards downhill from the shack.

"The boys' mother abandoned the family and ran off to live in the city; but they had a grandmother living with them. The grandmother often told Rosemary that Jesus was coming to save them; not today; but someday. The family was too poor to buy soap, so the grandmother saved up lard and fat drippings. She mixed those greasy drippings and some baking powder into a pot and heated it to a melted paste. Then she cooled it until it hardened; and broke the pieces into chunks which they used for soap. The family bathed sparingly; only when they could no longer stand their own smells. They washed in the creek behind the house. The creek was fed by a cold-water mountain spring. Rosemary remembers that freezing cold creek. She hated bathing in it; but the grandmother

made her bathe often, to wash away the boys' semen. The grandmother didn't want the family dogs sniffing around Rosemary, trying to hump her. And she didn't care for the dogs peeing on her mattress.

"The family simply threw its nonperishable trash beyond the cleared area in the back of the house. Rosemary remembers living with rats. The rats mostly stayed at the dump, but they constantly explored for food. Sometimes they got into their shack."

Frank: *"Sounds like she lived in a pig stye."*

John: *"Pretty much. The family had several pigs and chickens. They bred them and ate them. Pigs and chickens often got into the shack. Animals and people lived together in squalid, mish mash conditions.*

"Billy, Bart, and Brad were the family's boys. They were nasty to Rosemary. The father and grandmother let the boys abuse her; did nothing to stop them or protect her. The boys hit her and pinched her and fingered her and sodomized her from the time she was given to them until she was much older."

Frank: *"How did she survive a life like that?"*

John: *"She said she compartmentalized the things they did to her. She told herself that her mind was hers and no one could touch it because it was inside her skull where they couldn't get to it. And she read a lot; read whatever newspaper or magazine she could get her hands on. And she loved school. She had a teacher who liked her and let her take books home with her.*

"One book was about botany. That got her fascinated with plants. She read all about them. That's what started her thinking of herself as a grape plant. She believed that the more the boys stressed her, the deeper her root went

into her inner soul, her self-protective mental bedrock; until her mind learned to use her sexual abuse to direct its thinking and focus it. She trained her mind to mentally block out what was happening to her. She claims her abuse made her mentally tougher; and a better thinker and questioner. Abuse became a kind of mental nourishment. It helped her step into her inner self and to think of other people as outside dwellers who could only know her outer self; but never see her real self. That's what helped her understand why people did the things they did; why she became interested in human behavior. It's why she examined religion and why she questioned it and why she concluded that all religions are crazy.

"She became used to the brothers' sex play, if anyone can get used to that sort of stuff."

Frank: *"So, she became promiscuous?"*

John: *"No, she was never like that herself; but promiscuous women fascinated her. Human slavery better describes Rosemary's situation when she was a young girl. She told Sam that she started doing fellatio on the boys when she was about six or seven and taking their vaginal penetrations from when she was nine or ten. When she wasn't being made to work, the boys used her for sex; like she was their toy human sex slave. They treated her like they owned her and had rights to have sex with her.*

"The boys were never reprimanded. The father and grandmother didn't seem to think there was anything wrong with the way the boys treated Rosemary. She learned to cope with her abuse by appreciating her own mind. That's why she's so strong willed. She doesn't care what anyone thinks of her, or her writings. She writes for her own self-satisfaction, and she doesn't care whether

anyone else ever reads anything she's written. If you ever meet her, she'll strike you as unusual. She's resolutely independent; thoughtful; measured, not impulsive. And she speaks her own mind, or she says nothing. If you annoy her, she'll simply turn her back on you and walk away from you; or if it's a phone conversation, she'll simply hang up on you. It's not that she dislikes you. She just doesn't tolerate people who prattle on and on about banalities. Sam thinks Rosemary has a genius mind. He thinks her I Q is somewhere north of 160, way out in the high-end fringe tail of the human I Q distribution. Sam says Rosemary raised her acumen by training her mind to abstract the sex stuff; compartmentalize it."

Frank: *"You mean she started to enjoy it?"*

John: *"No, not in the way people who love each other enjoy sex. But she learned to accept sex as just part of living, like eating; and as something she was just expected to do. Sam said she started to consider sex as something that was simply a matter-of-fact part of her everyday life. She didn't seek it; but she learned not to dislike it or try to fight it, either. It just was. So, she accepted it. But while it was happening to her, she learned how to ask herself questions about why people think about other people in the ways that they do. How people think has fascinated her from an early age. She began noticing the differences in others, especially the three boys.*

"The middle boy was the most sensitive of the three. He started going with Rosemary when she bathed. He took a dry towel along and wrapped her in it when she finished. He didn't want her to catch cold. That boy was Rosemary's inspiration for one part in one of her Series books, THE BUTTERFLY YOU LOVE©. Her character,

Marty, discovers that a girl's sexuality exerts a mysterious control over boys. Marty uses that control to make one twin boy jealous of the other. Her seduction technique captures one twin's heart. He becomes one of Marty's lifelong lovers.

"Later, when Rosemary was in high school, one of her teachers told her that she had wealthy cousins. She traveled to Florida and looked up Sam. They became good friends and confidants. Sam put her through college. She really appreciated that. She thrived. She studied psychology and history; read many books. She loves reading books; learning what other minds think about things. She worked at understanding what kinds of people she wanted to include in her life and what sorts of people she wished to exclude.

"Understanding the limbic effect upon the human mind drives much of Rosemary's thinking. She believes that human intimacy is driven by natural limbic forces. And, as such, those activities are forms of necessary and sacred behavior, even when prostitution for money is involved. And, as such, those activities must not be forbidden, or proscribed by rules or laws, or made illegal or castigated in any way. Sam said she also studied religion because it has such a huge influence on peoples' lives and behaviors. She came to the opinion that religions cause more problems than they solve.

"Take Jews, for example. They say they are chosen people. But Rosemary asks: Who says so? Who tells you that? How can you prove it? She asks good questions. Why do the Jews believe those tales that started the Hebrew belief system? How do those homilies serve the Jews; make them believe that everyone who is not a

Jew is not chosen? And what does that mean? Does that mean that they are superior to other people; that they have a God-given right to use other people? What does that kind of thinking lead to?

"Then take Christians, especially Catholics. When a priest says you are not worthy to be called to the feast of the Eucharist, what does that mean? Who says you are blessed if you are called? And what does it imply if you are not blessed? Does that mean you are cursed? And who says a baby is born into sin? Really? Can you look at a baby and see its sins? Why would you believe those things? Are you really supposed to believe that you need to be meek; turn the other cheek? Where does that get you in life? And what makes you believe you had the right to murder millions of Native Americans, Jews, and Muslims; peoples of other faiths? What makes you think you have the right to force them to think your way; take their children from them to be trained into Catholicism? What does that kind of thinking lead to? How do you think the American Indians felt about it? Do you think they believed their genocide experience was a happiness?

"Muslims are another case. What gives them the right to kill people who think the Islamic way is not the right belief system for them? Who are they to say someone else is an infidel? And what if someone is one whom they consider to be an infidel? So what? What if two women like each other sexually? So what? She asks who appointed these clerical people to judge everyone else? It's the same kind of thinking that the other religions have, that it's okay to kill people who disagree with the way you think. Where does this kind of thinking come from? It's barbaric thinking. It results in people getting killed. And for what?

What good do those killings do? They only beget more killings. They don't change human nature.

"She believes all religions are rooted in barbaric thinking and all religions oppress women and squash their natural rights. People obediently follow these religious teachings and belief systems because they are taught as little children to believe that way. But it's all mind control by testosterone fueled, power crazed males. And to make their agendas work, religious leaders pan other religions; some even tell their followers that the other religions are bad. The leaders who spew this stuff exert inordinate psychological control over their followers. It keeps millions of people mired in an intractable psychological rut while the world passes them by. It produces a subtle form of mass insanity. It's groups of believing people going nuts, losing their humanity while marginalizing other peoples.

"Parts of Rosemary's work questions religious dogma. She created a saga filled with great stories about romantic loves and relationships. Her stories promote human love and kindness. They advocate for probative thinking about relationships, human-to-human connectivity and above all, deeply felt, true love. She explains the hidden allegorical meanings behind the homilies in the religious texts. Sam thinks her books should be taught in social studies classes at the senior high school and college levels. They give needed perspective. They open peoples' minds to the intentions of the original writers of religious texts, when they first reduced oral tradition to writings.

"If we could talk to Rosemary, I think she'd tell us that she believes in intimate Pagan ceremonial lovemaking. And I think she'd tell us that we are all living reincarnations of souls that have lived previous lives. There's also

her fascination with butterflies and all the analogous ways our reincarnated souls intersect the life cycles of the butterflies."

Frank: *"But that resurrection stuff is just theology. Butterfly spiritual transformations can't be true, can they? Is this a new theology, or is it fiction."*

John: *"Well, according to Rosemary, it's the reemergence of original, pre–Western religious theology. Pornography is leading a modern-day return to Pagan Asherah worship. It's human truths breaking free. It acknowledges that the free-spirited limbic mind can't be subjected to the rational frontal lobe-controlled mind; that both parts of the human mind need their own space and time in every human's life. It's an intriguing concept.*

"What's different now, thanks to the internet and mass media, is that we no longer worship at tribal prostitution ceremonies in places like Baalbek and Gobekli Tepi. Instead, we have lights and cameras, seductive messaging, and porn sets to stage our modern-day worshiping. We participate in individual viewer worshipping on an ad hoc, viewing it whenever we like, basis. But the underlying messaging is the same as it has been for twenty thousand years. Cousin Sam says what you hear from the lips of Ms. Sweets are the same words that came from Asherah, Astarte, Athena, Aphrodite, Eve, Sara, Bathsheba, Salame, Cleopatra, and Isabella. You hear the lure of Pagan intimacy. It seduces the limbic mind. It's compelling and it's irresistible."

Frank: *"But not all those women persuaded men to surrender their souls to them; even murder for them. Eve, Sara, and Isabella were religious women."*

John: "Nah. You're just taught to believe those stories without questioning them. But none of what you've been taught is true. All of those women relied upon Pagan intimacy to bend the world to their liking. Rosemary's work helps you think and see everything in a whole new light."

Frank: "A more permissive, mind-expanding light, right?"

John: "Oh, absolutely! Her work is much more allegorical. It makes you think. She gives many example stories which take judgmental religious homilies and puts them into mouse jars."

Frank: "Like how?"

John: "Well, take the story of Salame and John the Baptist, for example. Rosemary says something like that truly did happen. But the Gospel's homily is designed to misdirect the meaning of the story."

Frank: "What does Rosemary say about its true meaning?"

John: "Salame was not just a dancer. She was a Pagan temple goddess and a seductress extraordinaire. Men, including the King, worshipped her. They didn't just make love with her. They adored her. They worshipped her fornications; her fellatios; her sensational orgasms during cunnilingus; her orgies. They revered her and applauded her and handsomely rewarded her for her wantonness. And they considered her whoring to be a divine, sacred blessing for the Kingdom. Salome was among the world's first notorious, widely renown porn stars. She held the King's affections and his court's adoration, as well as their penises, in the palms of her hands.

"Suddenly, from the wilderness appears this unkept, locust eating, spit-spewing madman who screams that everything Salame does with the King and his court *is wrong and immoral. John the Baptist represents the world's original thought police. He represents western religion, with all its restrictions on thoughts and deeds. He represents the 'Thou Shalt Not' Commandments. The Baptist's religious way of thinking was inconceivable and laughable to Salame and the King. The Baptist's prescription for social order would eliminate the need for Salome's glorious pornography. It would ban her and other prostitutes like her from the kingdom. It would also destroy an important source of revenue for the King. What the Baptist advocated for the Kingdom's social order was, to Salome and the King, unfathomable lunacy.*

"Naturally, Salame wasn't having what the Baptist was selling. The world was already ordered very much to her liking, exactly the way it was. Naturally, she didn't wish to have her world disturbed. She didn't want thoughts about a different world order to gain adherents and take root. So, while Salome was joyously fornicating with the King, she told him that she wished to be pleasured in a newer, more creative, and decisively titillating way. She told him that she wanted the head of her detractor removed from his body and given to her as her King's affirmation that her pornographic displays and her insatiable appetite for wanton whoring were the triumphant, unquestioned, unassailable moral standards of the King's Kingdom. She demanded that her salacious debauchery be affirmed; and that her detractor be dealt the most severe rebuke: death. The King adored Salome. He loved her. He was smitten by her promiscuous charms. He gladly obliged her.

"After the Baptist was beheaded, Salome's agitation was assuaged. Thereafter, she was more relaxed while performing her breathtaking debaucheries. Her pornographic

performances were more spectacular than ever before. By virtue of her unrestrained wantonness, she became an international sensation. Great harmony for the King and his Kingdom ensued. Many Kings from neighboring nations brought gifts to the King and to Salome so that they, too, might indulge in Salome's delightful pleasures. Salome gladly obliged them with her unrivaled titillations; and sensational fornications and orgies. She was worshipped, exalted, and glorified.

"Christ needed to wait his turn to be praised. The King, in effect, became Salome's pimp. Both the King and Salome were greatly enriched. They became wealthier than they ever imagined possible. Their lives were early examples that immorality and pornography can be highly profitable career venues, and conduits for peaceful, harmonious relationships.

"Rosemary's works advocate for society's loving care, pampering, and deference to the needs of its prostitutes and porn stars. She opines that, through pornography, humanity attains greater harmony and tranquility. She often presents prostitution and pornography as vital countervailing social influences to the pompously righteous legions of religious thought police and their testosterone addled leaders."

Frank: *"But that is in total opposition to the way societies are presently structured."*

John: *"Yes. And here we are, on the brink of nuclear wars. Maybe we need to rethink things before we all kill each other and there's nobody left. Rosemary opines that humanity's limbic tranquility is essential for world peace; and that religions need to be seen objectively, as the dangerous adversaries to humanity's freedom that they really are."*

Frank: "It's hard to comprehend that humanity is on the verge of destroying itself because we cannot agree on the way to comprehend the female pussy."

John: "It is, isn't it? That's why Rosemary's work is so refreshing. She helps people recognize that promiscuity in the world around us is simply a natural expression of freedom. And that freedom is humanity's naturally desired condition. Sex shouldn't be criminalized; except children and innocents should never be brutalized. Her books give people great mental comfort. They are refreshing."

Frank: "You mean she's okay with porn, prostitution, and immoral liaisons, right? But not okay with murder, rape, or theft, right?"

John: "Yes, with a few exceptions. She condones the immoral behaviors of adultery and illicit liaisons. She explains those in terms of the amygdala and its reptilian grip on the limbic mind. She thinks pornography is the harbinger of humanity's return to Paganism and she sees that as a wonderful thing. But murderers receive punishment in her books. She distinguishes those who take human life as evil doers. They realize unimaginable consequences for their murders. Those story segments fit the horror genre. They are also wildly salacious."

Frank: "This Rosemary author treats the human amygdala as if it's the same as a reptilian's amygdala? So, a lot of what she writes is pretty raw?"

John: "Yes, but it's provocatively raw. Just like the sun's warmth heats up a reptile's amygdala and gets it moving to hunt food and to mate, that same gland produces the same hormones in humans. But in humans its hormones make us crave sexual pleasures. Rosemary's characters become controlled by their stimulated amygdala glands. Their *limbic minds possess them. Their ways of thinking about love and romance are different than the ways a rational mind thinks about these things.*

"Rosemary's characters think and relate in limbic terms. This unleashes surprising creative forces and unanticipated behavioral twists. Rosemary believes that God wanted this human limbic effect to happen. It's the 'go forth and multiply' commandment. God evolved us to include this facet of reptilian life so that humans would be highly sensitized to sexual stimulation. But God wanted humans to stay blind to the powers they had when the reptilian amygdala becomes stimulated. That's why God told Adam and Eve to stay away from the tree of knowledge. It's why a serpent reptile is used in the scriptures to persuade Eve to eat the fruit of the tree of knowledge and share its fruit with Adam. The serpent removed the scales from the eyes of Adam and Eve. They discovered sexual pleasures and thereby became God-like. They realized they could enjoy sex without having to procreate. Thereafter they no longer had any need for God. Humanity became God."

Frank: *"So, is Rosemary saying that a woman who knows how to stimulate a man's amygdala can induce within him a limbic mind-set which then controls his behavior?"*

John: *"Yes. Exactly right! Take the story of John the Baptist and Salome. Scripture portrays Salome as evil. But Rosemary portrays her as an advocate for the divinity of humanity. Rosemary sees Salome's whoring as humankind's glorious liberation from the constraints of rigid religious doctrine. Salome, an enticing, glorious Pagan whore, asserts herself as the only God that the King and his court need to sustain their happiness, peace, and well-being. When you can see the world in the same way that Rosemary does, a whole new world opens up for you. You'll then see this power shifting taking place all around you in everyday life.*

> *"Take Pete's situation. It's a perfect study of what Rosemary is trying to communicate to humanity. When you watched District Attorney Coglin give his opening, what did you feel?"*

Frank: *'Well, I felt anger and distress. I wanted to redirect that anger towards Pete; find him guilty and crucify him"*

John: *"Okay. Now, when you watched Marcy Adams give her opening, what did you feel?"*

Frank: *"Oh, well, that's a little harder to explain. I kept noticing how beautiful she was; her fresh, confident face; her shapely body; and those legs. She has spectacular legs."*

John: *"Yes, that's what you noticed. But what did you feel?"*

Frank: *"I felt charmed; like I wished there was some way that I could meet her; get to know her; hopefully bed her and fuck her until I could no longer think or see straight."*

John: *"Exactly. Well, there you have it. You see, if the District Attorney wins the case, it will not be because he has the better facts. It will be because he arouses anger in the frontal cortex lobes of the jurors' minds. He will win because he appeals to their sense of injustice and the logical follow-on that the murders must be made right."*

Frank: *"By convicting Pete and putting him to death. The death penalty, right?"*

John: *"Yes, the death penalty. But if Marcy Adams wins this case, it will be because she has successfully ignited the amygdala gland of one or more jurors, probably among the male jurors. The stimulated amygdala will ignite a juror's limbic passions. Those limbic passions will persuade that juror to acquit Pete because he knows an acquittal verdict will please Marcy Adams. That juror would allow the murders to go unpunished in order to please Marcy Adams. He hopes that by pleasing her she will be willing to meet him; get to know him; share the pleasure of her victory with him; and hopefully reward him with intimacy. He feels compelled to do whatever he can do to please her."*

Frank: *"Like how I felt when I looked at her?"*

John: *"Yes. As a man feels compelled to please a woman; exactly the same way."*

Frank: *"So, logic has nothing to do with how this jury will decide?"*

John: *"Not if you understand what Rosemary is telling you through her work. You see, she understands how the human mind really works. After you read her books, you will also gain that understanding. You'll have a life changing eye opener. It will change your perspective about many interactions you see in everyday life. Did you notice how Marcy Adams lingered before that one male juror in the front row of the jury box?"*

Frank: *"Yes, I noticed."*

John: *"Okay, good. Well, I promise you, that was not by accident or a lapse of her mind. That was deliberate. Marcy Adams was putting some heat under that juror's amygdala. She was persuading that little gland to take control of his limbic mind and his decision. She was making his limbic mind succumb to her charms."*

Frank: *"To entice him and flip him? To make him want to acquit?"*

John: *"Right. It only takes one juror to hang the jury. Our Marcy Adams, defense attorney, may be young and sweet and innocent looking; but she's no fool. She knows exactly what she's doing."*

Frank: *"So you think they will acquit Pete because Marcy Adams flipped one juror?"*

John: *"I don't know. Perhaps that juror is fantasizing that Marcy Adams is a thoroughly immoral porn star. Perhaps he fantasizes that she might become enthralled with pleasuring his penis. We'll have to wait for the verdict to know. Why don't you read Rosemary's Secret Butterly Series™? Then you'll have a better insight into such things. Your predictive skill set will vastly improve."*

Frank: *"Okay, so back to our Ms. Sweets, our notorious porn star. She is heating up Sam's amygdala. Am I getting this right? She is doing the proverbial time-tested seduction game with Sam, right? She's essentially fucking her way into half of his estate and getting him to finance eighteen feature length films which will rocket her to stardom, right?"*

John: *"Yes, she is doing all of that. But she's also got genuine affinity for Sam. Many porn stars have genuine feelings for their lovers. And many porn stars have multiple lovers. It's a natural humanistic way of life. And Ms. Sweets' and Sam's minds do think alike as far as her porn goes. She's fucking him for his money and her path to greater glory. He's along with all of what she does because he enjoys her way of thinking. The two of them think alike; and he enjoys the sex. Ms. Sweets is a highly motivated adult actress. She's driven to become the most notorious performer in her field and the most highly compensated. She wants to become the world's most glorified whore. Sam wants her to succeed. The two of them are a match made in heaven."*

Frank: *"Sweet Jesus. You're making it sound like Ms. Sweets got to Pete. You've got me thinking Pete could have done those murders."*

John: *"I don't think he did. Pete would have come to his senses."*

Frank: *"That makes sense. But I just don't figure old Sam. He should know better. How many times has he told us that America is a shining beacon to the world? How many times has he professed that we are the stellar example to the world; that Americans are the moral, decent, honorable, ones. This marriage to Ms. Sweets, porn star, seems to turn all of Sam's values on their heads. How does it figure that a man who is a pillar of the community, the very symbol of moral rectitude, suddenly betrays everything he professed to believe all his life?"*

John: *"I think America stays as the shining beacon to the world, regardless of how many people love their porn stars or how immoral Americans become. With all the nuclear weapons America has, no other nation would be foolish enough to challenge our supremacy. Actually, I think the more freedoms people have; the more we embrace immorality as a viable alternative to rigid moral codes, the brighter our beacon will shine. I think Sam understands this. He's only human like the rest of us. It's not hard to explain his thinking. Many men lead dual lives. Their public persona is one thing; but privately, they secretly consort with prostitutes. It's fairly common behavior; nothing to be ashamed of. It unleashes the amygdala's need for stimulation and satisfies the mind's natural limbic cravings.*

"Anyway, somehow Ms. Sweets became acquainted with Sam. Maybe she's a purely evil narcissist. Maybe she charmed Sam; got into his head; played a vulnerable

old man for his money? Maybe they connected mentally, like Sam says they did? Maybe they truly love each other, like Sam says they do. But think about this: Maybe there's something deeper going on? Sam's always been smart. He's scary smart. Sam's mind has always been flexible. And Sam has always had a nose for money. Maybe Sam sees something?"

Frank: *"Like what? A hot pussy?"*

John: *"Yes, that's for sure; but that's not what I mean. Maybe Sam senses that times are changing; that America's morals are changing. Maybe Sam sees that for America to remain that shining city on the hill, it's morals need to change to fit humanity's needs? Maybe he sees that our society, as it is presently configured, cannot dominate the world much longer? Maybe he sees that religion won't have its hold on public morality for much longer? Maybe he sees this Ms. Sweets woman as his entre' into making a killing on what's happening?"*

Frank: *"How?"*

John: *"This Ms. Sweets woman, Rosemary's Secret Butterfly Series™ books, the eighteen films, the sell through using virtual reality and artificial intelligence with Rosemary's characters, the licensed private clubs that will spin out of it. Who knows? Maybe Sam sees a hundred billion dollars. Don't ever underestimate him. He's nobody's fool. I had a talk with him about six months back. That was before he even met Ms. Sweets. He told me then that he saw America's morals changing. He said it might be a good thing for women to feel greater freedom about their sexuality; feel the freedom to have multiple lovers; be unashamed and unafraid to seduce and fuck a man when they feel like it.*

"The way Sam put it, he said it was time for women to remove the fig leaf and be unashamed of opening their eyes; time for them to leave the Garden of Eden; for real this time. He said it would soon be time to turn the hourglass over; time to let the sands of time flow out of religion and back into natural Paganism; back to before that day in the Garden when God started telling women what they should and should not do. He thinks it's time for women to tell God to take his rules of do's and don'ts and fuck off. He believes that religion, as we've been taught it and as we know it, is toast; and that pornography is humanity's new god. That's what's in Sam's head and he's going to run with it.

"He's excited about the film potentials of Rosemary's books. He wants to create the films in the same expressive narrative style of the classic French porn films of the mid 1980's. Like in those films, he wants the viewers to feel they are sharing the character lives of the women characters. They'll breeze through the stories' narratives, like the French porn stars did in their films; carefree, in natural, guiltless, joyful ways. The viewers will feel spontaneous empathy with the characters. They'll step into these women's shoes and walk with them in their lives. They'll feel the same intimate, romantic attachments that the actresses' characters develop. They'll feel their thrills, joys, exhilarations, and sexual conquests; their nuanced understandings of their relationships and love affairs; the fallings into their relationships and affairs, and their partings. But there will be one essential difference between the vintage French porn films and Sam's films. In the French films, the woman heroine is always cast as the one who is submissive to the male. That reflects the times when the films were made.

"But in Sam's films, the heroines may start out as submissives; but they use their wits and feminine wiles, and their ample applications of seductive sexuality to achieve independence, equality, and often dominance in their relationships with males. 'Rosemary's 'Susan' character's relationship with Marvin is a classic tale of feminine emergence from submissive to triumphant equality. It's a moving story. When I read the book, I first cried sad tears for Susan's impossible predicament; then, later, I cried happy tears for her glorious triumph.

"Sam's goal in this effort is to create the same carefree, nonchalant, natural, glorious promiscuity that you absorb from the French porn films, and incorporate that same accepted casualness in his American films; but with the films' orientations helping the viewer see the films' heroines, not as submissives like they are portrayed in the French films, but as equals and dominatrix's, or submissives evolved into dominatrix's, who are open and shamelessly unabashed about their sexuality. Sam believes the films will define our future male-female relationships in our new, more humanistic world.

"Another central character is Marty. Marty's character dominates her relationships from the outset. But Rosemary throws some Hitchcock-like twists into the plot lines of Marty's experiences. Marty is a diabolical woman. She is, first most, a lovable love. The reader cannot help but feeling deep empathy for her. Rosemary has her readers adoring Marty. Marty is caring, loving, incurably romantic, naturally promiscuous, sexually insatiable; and incredibly natural, and shameless about her lifestyle. And she has loves; deeply profound, emotive loves. But Marty can be mercurial and murderous. And she can murder

so innocently and understandably. I never would have believed I could empathize with and love a murderess, until I wrapped my mind around Marty's character.

"Rosemary places some intriguing plot twists into Marty's storied love affairs. A WOMAN'S VOICES(C), RUBY BUTTERFLY©, and later, when reincarnated Marty appears as Jen in TROPHY BUTTERFLY©, you'll feel amazement at the eerie, profound continuity of the femme seduction character, from Asherah, primitive temple goddess, through to Jen, with Marty, Susan, Cleopatra, Isabella, Delilah, Salome, Sara, Bathsheba, and all the lesser characters throughout the Series. It's harmonic; connective. The womanhood cravings and romantic needs in all these women resonates empathy, compassion, and love in your soul. It's an eternal love story. And, when I look at Pete's defense counsel, and how appealingly she presents herself, I cannot help but wonder whether she also understands the messaging that Rosemary has imparted to all women?"

Frank: *"What messaging?"*

John: *"That a woman does not have to be a helpless submissive to achieve equality in her relationships. She does not need to depend upon a male's approval to validate her. Equality or even dominance is hers for the taking, if she recognizes and applies her natural gifts and powers; becomes unafraid to lose her inhibitions; and confidently emboldens her love object to accept and love her as she wishes to be loved."*

Frank: *"That might explain why Sam's doing this. He sees how to capitalize on this changing perspective of feminine sexuality. His real driver actually isn't sex. It's money. He's going to adapt Rosemary's books as his baseplate; and create a breathtakingly beautiful film series that illustrates the changing power dynamics taking place in society. It will have a Renaissance-like effect; open peoples' minds. Viewers will love women more, if they're men; and they'll love themselves more, if they are woman.*

"Sam's smart. He's playing the money game. That explains why he won't care whether other men are penetrating his young wife. He'll love it. He'd see that as free publicity; attracting the paparazzi; good for business. People would talk about what a shameless, profligate, immoral whore his wife is. Yes, in Sam's mind, the more notorious a whore his new wife becomes, the better! And, like you said, he loves watching her fuck."

John: *"That all fits. Morality has nothing to do with it. With Sam, it's about the money. And watching Ms. Sweets fuck definitely stimulates male libidos. I have to agree with Sam's thinking here. Porn is definitely America's future. It's the fastest growing entertainment venue. As America's moral decay accelerates, porn, romantically themed and performed as casual, natural, shameless erotica, is destined to become the new standard in film craft. This new genre of porn films will receive adulation from all critics and interests. It will be embraced as breakthrough artistry; perfectly normal and natural; beautifully intimate human connectiveness; the ultimate, living achievement of artistic expression; appealing to both visual and auditory senses; stimulating, mesmerizing, spellbinding entertainment fare.*

"Sam mentioned his thoughts about licensing Rosemary's characters and her books in order to create an Artificial Intelligence version of Rosemary's SECRET BUTTERFLY SERIES™. He plans to make scripted

versions of the Series' scenes using voices he creates from real women's voices. The viewer will enjoy a realistic experience; vicariously make love with Rosemary's character, Marty, for instance. Think of the potential! Through virtual reality, viewers will vicariously experience making love with the world's most notorious porn star. He experiences hearing her innermost thoughts during their intimacy; hears her seductive, passionate voice expressing her feelings during foreplay and coitus; hears her thoughts about a lasting romantic involvement with him.

"Sam will offer an experience that far surpasses a real live date with a real live woman. When that customer views a new film release, he will expect to see his artificial intelligence dream girl performing live explicit romantic erotica scenes in that film. In order to have a successful film career, an actress will have to assume the persona of that artificially created dream girl. She will need to enthusiastically perform seductive porn scenes; and her performances will need to be exceptionally compelling and believable."

Frank: *"She doesn't need to be beautiful? Doesn't need a gorgeous body?"*

John: *"No, not really; not for males' limbic mind world. The physical beauty aspect of attraction isn't where eros happens. Eros happens inside the limbic mind. It's in that devilish little amygdala gland. A very plain looking woman can ignite that thing, set it ablaze, and make any man go totally crazy with lust for her. She can convince the man that she wants sex with him and that it's his greatest opportunity, ever, to have indescribably heavenly sex. She can master seduction artistry by watching porn. And she should. There's no better teacher.*

"Woman who master the art of seduction can pretty much have whatever they want in this world. I've been sensing that for a while now. It's not enough to be trained as an actress. Acting, per se, misses the point. It's seduction that titillates in film and in real life. Porn is what the public craves now; and successful actresses will deliver what the public demands. Women who resist this trend will not find work. They will fall by the wayside, like those actors and actresses who resisted performing in the early talking films fell by the wayside.

"The most highly accomplished, most seductive, and beguiling porn actresses will achieve stardom in this new era of film entertainment. Women who light up the audiences' libido while they seduce, copulate, and shamelessly express orgasm on screen will make a killing. And those women who are uninhibited, who love sexual intimacy, and who excel at enticing and seduction will achieve stardom and reap huge rewards. Theirs will become the personas that Sam adapts to his artificial intelligence created characters. They will perform as the Marty's, Susan's, and Sheila's of Sam's artificial fantasy world. Millions of intimacy-starved men will vicariously make love with their images. Uninhibited, profligate female actresses will prosper wildly by adapting their performing repertoires to our changing times."

Frank: *"I see. So, tell me, John, what is it about this SECRET BUTTERFLY SERIES™ that got Sam so interested? Why has he decided to produce it as eighteen films? What are they about? And what is it about our saucy Ms. Sweets that convinced Sam that she can play leading roles in several of these films?"*

CHAPTER FOUR

THE 'IT' FACTOR

John: *"The Series captured Sam's interest because the stories in the Series are exceptional romance novels. Sam loves salacious, erotic romance because it's so relatable to human feelings. He thinks Rosemary's work is masterful because it captures feeling.*

"He loves Ms. Sweets because of what he sees in her character. Ms. Sweets has that inner self. She has that 'It' factor. It's what comes through in her attitude. It's her inner immoral flame. It just comes through that cherubic face and vixen smile and those honest, healthy giggles that she bubbles, like effervescent champaign, while she's having sex. He loves how her eyes, mouth, face, and body express her carnal enjoyment while she copulates. He loves her mental attitude with respect to our society's moral degeneracy. She's among the first women in our new immoral era to openly express that it's perfectly normal and acceptable to engage in prostitution, pornography, and illicit liaisons.

"She's discovered that, in the world of new moral standards, it's regarded by many to be completely moral and acceptable to be immoral. She's completely at home in our new topsy turvey world. And she absolutely loves to fuck.

That's not an act. Her greatest delight is entertaining a male's penis. Her exhibitionist mindset aligns perfectly with her genuine proclivities to enjoy sexual pleasures. She's shameless and proud about her natural wantonness. She thinks conventional morality is an antiquated joke. She doesn't care one wit what anyone thinks of her licentiousness; pays no heed to the morality police. She's also into fashion; knows all the latest designs and haute couture; loves apparel and accessories that show off her body. Sam has always had an eye for women who display flash and class.

"Sam has a keen mind. He studies people and their characters extensively. He used a porn site that ranks porn stars based on their viewership and membership appeal. He studied several films from each of the top hundred ranked porn stars. Sam became attracted to Ms. Sweets. He noted that she put a great deal of credible feeling into her erotica. He fixated on one of her films. In that particular film, her porn performance was preceded by a soliloquy where she expressed gratitude for her fans' support. She also expressed how much she loved performing classic porn. She explained that there are costs involved in producing porn films. Then she implored her fans to continue supporting her because she loved performing her classic porn and she wished to continue providing her fans with more of her spectacular pornography.

"Well, old Sam watched that film many times. He told me the more he watched that film, the more he wanted her. In one film she made the comment that she didn't believe she had any special talent. That's what piqued Sam's interest in her. He thought she couldn't be more mistaken about herself. Sam sees her unique talent as a

brightness that shines out from within her inner self. She's confident, uninhibited, shameless, loving; enthused with her porn craft; open to trying new techniques and methods. And Sam adores her facial expressions and the way she carries herself. He especially loves the way her face lights up and her eyes become animated while she's being initially penetrated. That convinced him she had the 'It' factor.

Frank: *"This 'It' factor? What is it? Does every woman have it?"*

John: *"Well, observe Ms. Sweets' films. In the opening minutes, she's often portrayed as desirable, but somewhat elusive; forbidden, but tempting. It's all in her mannerisms; how she's alluring, seeming to be in control of her situation; yet vulnerable to her partner's romantic interest.*

"In Rosemary's Susan character, Susan is first portrayed as a helpless, entrapped innocent girl; yet she represents an enigma to Marvin. She personifies everything his wife is not. She's subservient, obedient, and gracious while wife Eloweiss heaps abuse on her. But chafing beneath Susan's external demeanor yearns a passion thirsting soul. She is much like a spring Daffodil, yearning to break free of her imprisoning ground, eager to display her spectacular glorious beauty. On the fateful Spring evening, she gives Marvin a peek of forthcoming delights by plumping her inviting breasts upward and outward. The elusive, forbidden damsel suddenly ignites Marvin's amygdala. Susan ensnares his limbic mind, never to relinquish her control of it. Later in their affair Susan reveals her outer edge. Like a piercing swordlike Daffodil leaf, Susan cuts deeply into oppressive Eloweiss. Susan thrives as her promiscuity broadens to ensnare corporate chieftains, union bosses, and charming Colonel Juan Peron.

Her character understood behaviors of men and women. Her 'It' factor understood how her own behavior could ignite the male amygdala. Women who read Susan's story may see elements of themselves in her situation. If they desire to emulate her successes, they may decide to adopt some of her tactics.

"Marty's character is shaped by abandonment and rejection issues. Much like her mother, Susan, Marty resents her situation. But unlike Susan, who relieves her frustrations by seducing Marvin, Marty internalizes hers. Initially, it's stones. She imagines white pebble stones are her lovers. But here she develops an extraordinary 'It' factor. She trains her limbic mind to become numb to love. She drops a stone when she becomes tired of it; and she picks up another stone to love. Marty hones her 'It' factor. She develops her character into that of a seductress extraordinaire. Boys and men are drawn to her sweet promiscuity. Males' involvement with Marty is like eating the fruit of the Deadly Nightshade plant; very sweet tasting, but fatal to life as they knew it. Men's wives, girlfriends, careers, and wealth are all destroyed by Marty, for she is a possessive, demanding lover. Her lust for conquest is insatiable. Even knowing this, men cannot resist her sweet charms. Women who desire being surrounded by men who bow before them and throw down their lives at their feet, may wish to emulate Marty's character.

"Barbara, the Native American Lakota girl, is another study of the 'It' factor. She was born of an Arab mother and Indian father. After her mother's death, she was raised by her father and taught to think like men and wild animals think. Her tribal roots impressed upon her the need to serve the people of her tribe. Unlike Susan and

Marty, she seeks to give love, never to take love. This difference in perspective about love enables selfless Barbara to play the long game of love, and win it. Her story is a lesson in determination, loyalty, duty, and honor. After a series of bizarre twists, Barbara ends up having it all. If a woman's goal is to have a sincere, loving family life, she would do well to emulate Barbara's character.

"These three women have different individual variations of the essential 'It' factor. The interplay between these three; how they navigate each other's boundaries; how they function and carve out their own spaces within David's twisted character ordered world offers women a study of business acumen and success. Recognizing another woman's 'It' and knowing how to relate to her opens doors of essential understanding and perspectives people don't get from 'how to do it' books.

Frank: *"So, different women can have different 'It' factors. I get it. It's some kind of latent desire that all women have, right? But do all women have it?"*

John: *"Yes. All women have it. But it's not well understood. When you understand Susan and Marty, you'll see that it can express in complex ways. Unfortunately, most women try to suppress their 'It.' When you understand Barbara, you'll see that some women have extraordinary patience, knowing that they have 'It,' while containing 'It' before they finally unleash 'It.' Then, 'It' can be spectacular. Highly promiscuous women, like Marty, and later characters, Connie, and Jen, recognize that they have 'It' and try to capitalize on 'It' throughout their relationships. It's most apparently obvious in women who have no shame in expressing their nympho tendencies."*

Frank: *"I don't understand."*

John: "That's because you're a guy. Maybe it would help you understand if you made love with Ms. Sweets."

Frank: "And you did? You made love with Ms. Sweets?"

John: "Yes…. Once." John averted Franks eyes. His shoulders shrugged. He felt a little sheepish.

Frank: "Well, then, describe 'It' for me."

John: "Okay. Well, it's not how I felt while making love with other women."

Frank: "No?"

John: "No. It's different. Your world and her world become one world. It's like you've become plugged into something that's both immoral and immortal. Like, she holds you in tightly while she's thrusting her mons into your penis, devouring it; then slowly, seductively retreating her mons; while writhing the entire time, recalibrating her enthusiasm for her next thrust. While making love with her, there's no yesterday and no tomorrow. There's only today; only now; only those precious, memorable moments while you're with her.

"You have this awareness that she's got her nails dug into your back and your ass so you can't move away; like she needs to hold you in tightly so she can take all the semen and sperm you have away from you and into her. And you don't care about the pain her nails are imparting to you. They stimulate you to love her more deeply. You tune out the pain. And you lose your soul into her. And while she got you all wrapped up into her like that, she kisses you and puts her eyes right up close against your eyes. I swear, Frank, I went into other worlds while she did that."

Frank: "What do you mean?"

John: *"Well, it was sublime and eerie at the same time. I never wanted to stop fucking her; like I wanted to fuck her until I died from fucking her. I swear, our lovemaking was so wonderful, I didn't care if I had a heart attack and died from it. I would have rather had the heart attack and died than stop making love with her. It was like I imagined myself fluttering with her."*

Frank: *"You mean like a butterfly?"*

John: *"Yeah. It was like, for a while there, while I was releasing all my semen, I became like one of those Monarch butterflies. I was fluttering with her in mid-air. We were high above the canopy of the Mexican jungle. My penis was deep inside her vag, like it had become my eternal receptor. I needed to stay inside it and give it every last drop of semen I had inside me. I felt like she was taking my very life away from me; but I didn't care. I couldn't stop. I felt like this is what I was meant to do with my life. I was loving what she was doing. And I loved her in this eternal sort of way. It was unlike I've ever loved any woman before her. I had this feeling like she deserved to have my life essence; like it was her right to take it from me. The two of us were creating new life inside her; inside her holy of holies place."*

Frank: *"You mean inside her vulva? You mean you were deeply into her cunt and shooting your pasty cum into her vulva?"*

John: *"Oh yeah. But something else started happening; something that has never happened between me and any other woman."*

Frank: *"What was it?"*

CHAPTER FIVE

KNOWING ETERNITY

John:	*"It was her eyes, Frank. It was like her eyes were suddenly looking into my eyes from behind butterfly wings. I had this transformational experience. Her eyes took my soul away from me and stole it away into eternity with her. I knew I was experiencing something spiritual; holy. I knew I would never get my soul back. I knew I had lost control of it. She had it. She wanted it and she took it. And I didn't care. I wanted her to have it. I wanted her to devour it and make it become a part of her.*

"When I looked into her eyes, I saw these vivid scenes from history. I could see these historic femme fatales seducing their love interests and making love with them, in all sorts of different erotic settings. I saw Asherah, Astarte, Athena, Aphrodite, Venus, Eve, Sarah, Bathsheba, Salome, Cleopatra, Isabella, and several gorgeous porn stars from our recent past. And I saw all the female characters from the SECRET BUTTERFLY SERIES™ playing their roles in the Series. It was like watching the history of love and sex in triple fast forward; and all of it was happening inside Ms. Sweet's eyes. Only each individual scene slowed down and happened in slow motion, as if her soul began communicating directly with my mind;

showing my mind how spectacularly wondrous erotic intimacy is; how glorious lovemaking is; how precious it is that we, as humans, have this experience available to us. Time stood still while I made love with Ms. Sweets. Her eyes let me witness each of these femme fatales making love while she and I made love."

Frank: *"That's crazy."*

John: *"Yes. But I'm telling you the truth. I saw the most erotic scenes I've ever seen. It was real. My soul came alive and I lived in all those scenes with all those glorious femmes. I could feel what each of them were feeling. I felt their romantic passions and their unbridled, shameless lusts; and their spirits' eternal loves. My spirit soul made love with every one of these women while I was making love with Ms. Sweets. My soul cascaded through endless halls of empathetic, romantic love. I didn't want to return to our real world. I'm convinced: Ms. Sweets eyes are a window into all the historic past love affairs and boudoir seductions of the entire world's most famous seductresses."*

Frank: *"How can this be?"*

John: *"It's some kind of psychological phenomena. And it happens quickly, almost instantaneously. It's the switching on of the limbic control of the brain. It's caused by sudden stimulation of the amygdala gland."*

Frank: *"That's the reptilian fight or flight gland?"*

John: *"Yes, it's also found in reptiles. But in humans the gland has evolved to become ultra sensitized to sexual stimulation.*

Frank: *"You mean like when you see a porn star kissing her partner while simultaneously placing her hand on his penis?"*

John: *"Exactly. Those stimuli trigger an instantaneous response in the amygdala. The limbic mind switches on. It says: 'I love her. I want her. I must fuck her.' That's accompanied by a surge in blood flow to the penis. It's perfectly natural. The male mind cannot resist its overpowering force. It's the same force that captured Sam's imagination and his heart. He was already preconditioned to fall in love with a porn star after reading Rosemary Ness Bitner's books. He saw our sweet peach, our Ms. Sweets woman, as the living reincarnation of the female nympho characters in the 'SECRET BUTTERFLY SERIES™.*

"Sam thinks our Ms. Sweets woman was sent to him for the most wonderful journey of his life. When he noticed her, his limbic mind just took control of him. He had to have her. He obsessed over her. He studied every film she ever made. He decided that she was a sincere young woman who was speaking to him through her heart. He could tell she was passionate about her intense desire to perform exceptional porn. And he saw she has the kind of persona that is open to a mentoring coach and a team of assistants who will make her into an even more spectacular actress than she already is.

"Sam believes she carries within her eyes the messaging that will change the world. He now thinks religion has everything all wrong."

Frank: *"Which religion has everything wrong?"*

John: *"All of them. Sam thinks all religions have everything all wrong."*

Frank: *"I don't get it."*

John: *"Well, Sam thinks all religions are nothing more than control mechanisms; essentially vehicles that allow small cult-like groups of men to rule over people. He thinks these religious cult control freaks have distorted historical truths through their homilies which they codified into scripture. Sam says it's all bull shit."*

Frank: *"Why do you think religions got control of society in the first place?"*

John: *"Huge question. Likely, jealousy played a part. When humanity was Pagan and tribal, before religious laws, survival was organized around the hunt. After killing a mastodon, the members of the hunting party celebrated by fornicating with the tribal prostitute. The prostitute was the tribal member upon whom the tribe depended for their cohesiveness; to keep them bonded as one; thus, insuring their very survival. They needed her. They needed to honor her, pay homage to her, and satisfy her. Males' limbic minds of twenty thousand years ago needed the same reassuring messages of males' minds today: Love, unity of devotion; and confidence in the perpetuity of the human species through procreation. Today's porn stars uniquely fulfill that role of social unifiers because males know these women are there for them; they serve as social relief valves for human stress and acceptance, just as their prehistoric Pagan prostitute predecessors did. We even have awards for our porn stars. Much like our ancestors gave their tribal prostitutes mastodon tusks to adorn their caves, we give today's porn stars trophies for their most notable, outstanding porn performances. We applaud and glorify their fornications. We pay homage to them. We pay to attend their conventions. We clamor to have our photograph taken with them and we beg them for their autographs. We flow a steady stream of tribute to them in the form of money payments for advertising spots on their films, outright film purchases, endorsements, and private membership fees.*

"The older prostitution worshipping ways were not sustainable. Older Pagan men could not satisfy the

prostitutes' insatiable libidos like the younger men could; so, gradually, they twisted the bearded shepherds' stories into homilies which the elders of these tribes fashioned into religious rules. These rules were the wedge that opened the door to religion as we know it today. Eventually, the religions' elder leaders opined that prostitution worship was bad; and they restructured worship to honor an imaginary, abstract God to replace traditional Pagan prostitution worship."

Frank: *"And now, Rosemary thinks, this process is being reversed. We are returning to prostitution worship?"*

John: *"Yes. Her fictional work guides you by tracing humanity's evolving perspective of the female libido. You see, back in prehistoric times, before Lycopene, Ginko, Vitamin E, and the little blue pill, older males felt threatened by the powers of the younger males. Naturally, the prostitutes preferred a male between the ages of thirteen and twenty to a post-thirty-year-old male. But now, older males have those enablers and they are better able to satisfy the female libido; so, prostitution worship no longer poses the same threat to older males that it did before the twentieth century. Today's older males have much more parity with younger males than they did twenty thousand years ago; and they tend to have more money. Hence, they no longer feel threatened by the female libido's insatiable quest for satisfaction. Now, older males embrace the females' eternal quest. They encourage it by fully participating, along with the younger males. Rules forbidding prostitution and pornography are being ignored and swept aside. Enforcement of antiquated, religion inspired prohibitions is increasingly ignored."*

Frank: *"And Rosemary's fictional saga lays this out for us?"*

John: *"Yes; and in a very entertaining, understanding way which takes you through the emotional components of it; reveals the thoughts of the seductress, and her partners; those who observe her methods; those who try to intervene; and those who accommodate her. Rosemary uses her Marty character as a reincarnated woman who comes to us through twenty millennia. Marty's mind is the readers' guide for the journey through the Series. Her thoughts are revealed. You empathize with her romantic thoughts while she fornicates with her tribal warrior band after they kill a mastodon. You relate to her thinking and her needs as a biblical prostitute; a Salome, Sara, Bathsheba. Her emotions as Cleopatra and Isabella are revealed. And her more recent romantic desires are explored as she uses her highly refined libido and seduction talents to control her male partners, Daren, Carl, Fred, Big Ed, and the others; and get her what she wants. You feel her possessive impulses; her deeply seated need to be the love object of her partners. You'll also appreciate her narcissistic need to murder.*

"You'll also understand, by her experiences with the young men of her school years; through her later seductions of Bob, Marshawn, Dominick, and George, how a woman with a nympho mindset reasserts women's natural control over men and society as a whole. The profound significance of modern-day porn stars will become apparent. They are not a marginal underclass as our religions try to portray them. They extremely important women with highly refined libidos and exceptional, highly developed thought processes. They are not mindless cum dumpsters or brain-dead sluts. Au contraire! Those are disparaging toss off terms used by thought police to

denigrate exceptionally courageous, gifted women who possess uncanny social insights. These are sensitive, highly refined, often highly educated women who are remaking society's morality by returning our morality to its more natural humanistic condition. They are to be appreciated; not feared, or denigrated. They are leaders who need to be accepted as early practitioners of our new, modern-day form of prostitution worship.

"Pornography and its porn stars are not a passing fad, Frank. These women and the intimate artistry they perform are here to stay. Prostitution worship is in the process of reestablishing itself as a viable religion. It is in the early stages of retaking its rightful market share from established religions. It may help ease strife and tensions in our world. Think of it as a case study in business marketing. Understand it, accept it, and embrace it."

Frank: *"And this Ms. Sweets woman's eyes carry this truth, somehow?"*

John: *"Yes, Frank, that's what I'm telling you! Sam believes Ms. Sweets is an exceptional porn star. He sees her as the living antidote to the dead, and resurrected, Jesus Christ. He believes eternity has brought forward Ms. Sweets as the Antichrist; given her to us to be worshiped and adored. He claims she was sent to us to change the world. He thinks she was sent as a divine messenger to tell us that pornography is beautiful; that it's a new form of religion; and that humankind should convert to it. And she loves performing her conversions."*

Frank: *"You mean she loves to fuck, right?"*

John: *"Absolutely, she does. When you do it with Ms. Sweets, you'll see what I mean. Her eyes will reveal the truth to you. While you're doing her, look into her eyes. I mean*

*really hold her close and stare into her eyes while she
makes love with you. You'll see the truth, too. Her eyes
will reveal to you what actually happened throughout all
of human history. You'll see Asherah and Astarte doing
their pagan goddess fornications; biblical Terah making
incestuous love with his daughter Sara; and Sara making
incestuous love with her brother, Abram; Abram pimping
Sara to Pharoah; Sara doing prostitution with Pharoah
and his sons; Bathsheba's murder plots and whoring her
way to become King David's favorite wife; Salome's seductions and John the Baptist's severed head to acknowledge
Salame's immoral dominance, ensuring her peace of mind
and rightful place in the Kingdom; and many others.
They'll all flash before your eyes instantaneously, but your
mind slows them down to real time so you can comprehend what actually happened."*

Frank: *"You mean I'll live in a kind of time warp, so I can feel the
romance of each love scene?"*

John: *"Yes! It's amazing. You live past realities with the most
sensational seductresses of all time! You are be right there
while those seductions are happening. You'll be amazed."*

Frank: *"So, her eyes reveal the truth, you say. They'll tell me a
different, truthful version of historical events; essentially,
they'll debunk the biblical stories."*

John: *"Exactly right. They turn religion on its head. They'll
explain how Paganism is good and normal and the natural way to honor human life. You'll see. Ms. Sweets will
convert you. You'll become a humanist. You won't want to
go back to your old ways. You'll become a changed man.
You'll conclude that practicing a religion is not optimal for
your inner soul. After you've made love with Ms. Sweets,
you'll appreciate how the SECRET BUTTERFLY SERIES*

™ brings everything forward to our modern times. You'll love how the Series, with its revealing allegories, relates to historical events and corrects the historical record to reflect the true Pagan nature of humankind. You'll keep the SERIES' books by your bedside and refer to them for your answers to life's mysteries. You won't feel a need to have a bible anymore."

Frank: *"And Sam is really into this woman? This is for real?"*

John: *"Absolutely. After he studied that first film, Sam watched ten more of her films, several times each. He concluded that she had that special 'It' factor and that she wasn't faking it. The 'It' factor, for Sam, is something that must come from within a person. It's not how beautiful her eyes, skin, breasts, or legs are; although Ms. Sweets is indeed very beautiful in all those surface measurements of beauty. The 'It' factor is something that Ms. Sweets communicates through her body of work. She communicates that she loves performing her porn; that she's honored to perform it.*

"She personifies the majesty of a Pagan temple goddess; venerated and glorified in her whoring. She's living, beautiful artistry, Frank. That comes through to her viewers by the way she giggles and does her oohs and aahs when her partners pinch and bite her nipples; by the ways she shrieks and giggles and chortles while she becomes slippery wet inside; while cocks begin penetrating her; and while she orgasms. Sex releases immeasurable joys from within her. Her love of sex comes through the screen and enters your very soul. She captures your soul and binds it to hers.

"She's a human lifeline; a truth people can believe in; a refreshing antidote to their toxic social order. Their

frontal cortex-controlled minds yearn for truth, integrity, and leadership; but they cannot find it. Frustration! It receives no respite or comfort. Madness! Despair! It gives up. Seeking self-preservation, it surrenders its behavioral control. The limbic mind awakens; asserts itself, lifts the human spirit. The procreation spirit's soothing balm reassures the soul that humanity will persevere and survive. Ms. Sweets provides those vital stays. Copulating with her becomes salvation and rebirth. She, and porn stars like her, are the vital reassurance that binds human life to eternity. Our porn stars deliver needed soothing balm to limbic minds. They rekindle hope; reaffirm mankind's self-worth; and free the human spirit. Belief in the perpetuation of human kind is as needed today as it was twenty thousand primitive years ago.

"Ms. Sweets personifies humanity's capacity for change. She confronts the established order and makes it heel. And she's deliciously addictive. You'll want more of her. You'll be mesmerized by how she loves bantering with her partners. You'll see. She loves playing her roles and she loves all seduction art's alluring feminine aspects. She is an artisan who loves what she does; is completely at home within herself and her decision to create porn. She is joyous about delivering a premium porn product to her growing fan base. She's on a mission to spread her truth. And she's honest and accessible to suggestions that might help her become the world's premier artisan of erotica."

Frank: *"It's hard to understand why Sam would be attracted to a woman who performs obscenities."*

John: *"Define obscene."*

Frank: *"Well, like Justice Potter said: 'I'll know it when I see it.' It's something that repulses."*

John: *"Like the genocide of America's Native Americans and their buffalo?"*

Frank: *"Well, yes; definitely. But I was referring to explicit sex."*

John: *"Well, look at this film of her. She's lying on a bed while getting a massage. Is that obscene?"*

Frank: *"No; it's a prelude to obscenity."*

John: *"Okay. Well, the camera is shooting a view up her legs. It's revealing her vag. What thoughts go through your mind?"*

Frank: *"Well, while her partner was massaging her neck and shoulders and her torso and buttocks and leg muscles, I could not help but imagining the hundred or more penises that she has copulated with. I realized I was seeing the anatomy of a woman who is an incorrigible, wanton, fucking machine."*

John: *"Is that obscene?"*

Frank: *"Well, not yet."*

John: *"Okay. Well, now she's lying on her back with her legs spread. Her partner has begun performing cunnilingus with her Lady Lips. Is that obscene?"*

Frank: *"Yes. I think, maybe it is."*

John: *"Well, what happened in your mind from the time she was being massaged to now?"*

Frank: *"Well, it sort of changed. It went from being objective to being emotional. I felt this arousal. I felt like Ms. Sweets, with her partner, was taking me into a different sort of mental zone."*

John: *"I can help you here. That was your mind switching over to limbic mode. Your emotive responses to Ms. Sweet's antics began taking control of your mind. So, how did that scene make you feel?"*

Frank: *"A bit entranced; like I wanted to see more of her facial smiles and hear more of her moans for pleasure. I also* felt enticed, wanting to see her doing sexual things with a penis."

John: "Well, did that oral sex scene repulse you?"

Frank: "Not exactly. It's more accurate to say it shocked me."

John: "That was your mind adjusting to limbic control. But did the scene make you feel repugnance like seeing a field filled with Indian women and children who had been massacred; or the Great Plains littered with rotting buffalo carcasses?"

Frank: "No. I reviled at those scenes. I was disgusted. I felt like throwing up. But with Ms. Sweets offering her vagina for cunnilingus, I felt more awestruck than anything. I felt: 'Here is a gorgeous woman who has no shame in being pleasured with oral sex. Here is a woman who obviously feels oral sex is very natural and something to be enjoyed. And here is a woman who is uninhibited about displaying her joy of being pleasured; and who is unconcerned; immodest about sharing that joy with the cameras for all the world to see.' So, I guess I can't say I was repulsed."

John: "Good, Frank. We're making some progress here. Now, let's go a little deeper into the subliminal communication you were receiving from Ms. Sweets when she began performing fellatio on her partner's penis. Did you notice her facial expressions while she kissed it and licked it? Did you get a sense of what was going through her mind as she sucked it and stroked it?"

Frank: "Yes. I sensed that she loved the penis and she loved what she was doing with it."

John: "Loved it?"

Frank: "Well, yes. Even more than loved it. It seemed like she adored it; like she believed she was blessed by some spiritual force to be able to do those things with it."

John: *"Good, Frank. What you expressed about what you were sensing was what she was experiencing in her mind. Can you say that she believed what she was doing was obscene?"*

Frank: *"No. I think she believed what she was doing was heaven sent; something of a Godly nature; something beautiful and glorious."*

John: *"And your limbic mind, observing her performing as she was, also believed you were observing something heaven sent; of a Godly nature; and beautiful and glorious, didn't you?"*

Frank: *"Yes. I suppose I did. But that is completely at odds with what I'm supposed to believe. It contradicts what my religious and parental instruction told me. Those teachings instructed me to hold the opinion that what I was watching was dirty and obscene; that I was bad to be watching it; that Ms. Sweets was a woman possessed by Satan or something."*

John: *"Those beliefs were what your frontal cortex, unemotional, unfeeling mind was taught and trained about how to process that scene. But Ms. Sweets swept all that away when she smiled and bantered with her partner; when she told him how much she adored his penis, didn't she?"*

Frank: *"Yes. I admit it. She did. What happened in my own mind?"*

John: *"You succumbed to Ms. Sweets' charms; her sex appeal. Your limbic mind decided it needed to see more of what she was showing you; it needed to feel a closer bond with her. Isn't that true?"*

Frank: *"Yes. I felt like I needed to buy her films; join her private member service; meet her, and make love with her. My inhibitions about her being a whore; a porn star; a fallen woman, all my reluctance and discomfort about yielding myself, and my love and my money to her simply vanished; like suddenly, my resistance just left me and she remained. I wanted her. I mean, I craved her. I felt like I needed her."*

John: *"Good. That's all natural. Now, let's go one step further. We've established that you have a limbic mind. Would it surprise you to learn that Ms. Sweets also has a limbic mind?"*

Frank: *"No, of course not."*

John: *"Well, while she was performing her sensational fellatio, don't you think she was also aware that she was being filmed?"*

Frank: *"Sure she was."*

John: *"Okay. Well, what sorts of subliminal thoughts can you imagine were going through her mind while she kissed and stroked her partner's penis; and later, when she guided its penetration into her vagina?"*

Frank: *"Well, she obviously loved what she was doing. I mean, her face was all smiles. Her expressions signaled that she was obviously pleased with all the explicit sex she was participating in. She expressed verbal pleasure about how wonderful she felt; how much his pleasuring's pleased her; how thrilled she was to be his sex partner. I mean, she really put her heart and soul into her performance."*

John: *"Good, Frank. Now why do you think she was doing that?"*

Frank: *"Well, I suppose by being so enamored with their sex play herself, she caused her partner to feel enamored also; thus, making the performance that much more enticing and spellbinding."*

John: *"Okay. That's all true. But try to place your mind into Ms. Sweet's mind for a moment. What drives her to perform this way, film after film? You tell me. Think limbic in her mind; not yours."*

Frank: *"I'm stumped. Help me here. What's going on in her mind?"*

John: *"She's trying her utmost best to create a visual masterpiece. Think, Frank. She sees herself as an artist. And she is an artist, She's a performer of intimacy art. She's an artisan, a perfectionist of her craft. Her mind is driven to create the most exquisite, living pornographic art, ever. In this respect, her mind is no different than the mind of a Rembrandt, a Gogan, a Picasso, a Ruben. They all sought to inspire through their art.*

     "Ms. Sweets, likewise, seeks to inspire through her art. She seeks to set humanity free. She offers the best of her creative work to the world in hopes that she will inspire people to lose their inhibitions and love freely and shamelessly; without passing judgment upon one another for their natural seeking of freedom from religious and moralizing constraints. She expresses that there should be no taboos concerning human intimacy; that adultery should be accepted as a commonplace, normal, healthy, expression of limbic desires; that no one should cast stones upon the adulterers. So, with that perspective, do you still see her pornography as obscene?"

Frank: *"No, I cannot."*

John: *"Can you now see her, and all the other porn stars, as creative artisans?"*

Frank: *"Yes, indeed I can. You are converting my beliefs, aren't you?"*

John: *"Almost. Can you also see why the most acclaimed and successful porn stars are highly sought after, like a prized Rembrandt, or a Picasso?"*

Frank: *"You mean to acquire their films; join their private services; consort with them?"*

John: *"Yes. All that and much more. When you see Rembrandt's Mona Lisa, what thoughts do you have?*

Frank: *"I see a beautiful, sensuous woman. I think she is tempting me to come to her; a woman who, quite possibly, has just had a very satisfying sexual encounter; yet, she is uninhibited, ecumenical, and she also wants me to consort with her. I think I see a woman who can make love through all eternity and never be completely sexually satisfied. Also, I see a woman who knows she is adored and treasured. She knows she is special to the heart and soul of her lover, or lovers. The painting's background informs me that she was sent to Earth from the spirit realm; that she is divine womanhood, uniquely possessed with creation powers. She could be Eve, reincarnated."*

John: *"Well, Frank, you are expressing the same sorts of thoughts and feelings that Ms. Sweets has while she creates her pornography."*

Frank: *"And you know this? How?"*

John: *"By my conversations with her; getting to know her; listening while she expressed herself."*

Frank: *"Would you relate her conversations to me?"*

John: *"Sure. I started by asking her: Do you ever feel guilty about performing as a porn star?"*

MS.
Sweets: *"Oh, you're thinking about how religious types say I'm a bad girl, right?*

John: *"Yes, exactly."*

Ms. Sweets: *"Well, fifty years ago, people thought it was a good idea to smoke cigarettes. They believed smoking was good. They also thought it was healthy to give soft drinks to infants. Those beliefs turned out to be wrong. Times change. People change.*

"I think religion will go the way of the cigarette. Religion emphasizes what you should not do, and expects you to believe in mystical tales. It requires suspension of reality and common sense. That makes it work. That delivers the cash flows to the people at the top of the religions, the ones who make their livings professing it.

"People are becoming skeptical of the tales. The scientific method of thinking has caused an attitudinal change. Religion has been pushed off its throne. It doesn't hold the same moral high ground it used to hold. Many people are deciding religion is bad for their mental health. They are moving away from it; moving more toward pornography, because porn expresses the beauty of humanism. People need that. They don't want to hear about being born into sin or how their minds are filled with evil thoughts; or how people outside their religion are bad or unworthy. They'd rather believe in love. They accept that love exists in other people."

John: *"And porn gives them that belief?"*

Ms. Sweets: *"I think so. It's a release from religious authoritarianism and government control."*

John: *"Like drugs and alcohol?"*

Ms. Sweets: *"Better. Intimacy is not a depressant. It uplifts; gives hope. It demonstrates rebellion against orthodoxies that prevent people from thinking for themselves. It symbolizes humanity's awakening to the beauty of freedom. Believers in porn feel no need to conform. Porn understands that people are individuals. It accepts them as they are. There's no need to perform rituals to be accepted. Porn accepts everyone. When you watch my films, am I not accepting?"*

John: *"Yes, Ms. Sweets, you certainly are. What first got you interested in performing porn?"*

Ms.   *"I was introduced to it by my boyfriend at the time. His*
Sweets: *name was Brad. We were young; in high school, and we were in love and having sex. We even talked about getting married someday. I was fifteen. He was sixteen.*

"He took me to an adult theater to see a porn film. When it was over, he asked me if I'd suck his penis like the porn actress sucked penises. We talked about it. He revealed that he wished he could have sex with that particular porn actress and also be married to me. I told him he could either have me as his wife some day; or he could have relationships with porn stars and prostitutes; but that he couldn't have it both ways."

John: *"So, what did he do?"*

Ms.   *"He contacted the porn star and had sex with her. Then he*
Sweets: *wanted to come back to me; but continue seeing the porn star. That's when I told him we needed to break up. Eventually, he married another girl. Her name was Cynthia.*

"Meanwhile, I decided that, possibly, porn would be a good career path for me, since I very much loved sex. I went to a modeling agency. They created a portfolio of photos, posing me suggestively in different outfits and bikinis; also invitingly naked. They referred me to some production companies that produced porn films. I went to three studios and auditioned to perform porn. I was accepted by all three and contracted through my agent to create nine films. I was on my way. But here's the irony. Brad saw one of my films. He contacted me and wanted

to have sexual relations with me while being married to Cynthia."

John: "And you agreed?"

Ms. Sweets: "It seemed awkward. It was a complete role reversal. But it was what Brad wanted. I wasn't his wife. She was. So, I agreed. We had fabulous sex; even better than when we were dating and in love. But I had to stop seeing him."

John: "Why?"

Ms. Sweets: "Well, I would have continued our liaison. I would have been his relief from monogamy. But Brad wanted more than that. He wanted to marry me and divorce Cynthia. By this time, I was a budding porn star, enjoying my career. I didn't want anything to do with marriage. I told him: 'No.' I told him he didn't understand what it means to be married; that it takes commitment to the other person. I told him he was free to divorce Cynthia; that that would be perfectly fine with me. He was also free to continue seeing me. But I told him I would not marry him. I told him the kind of relationship I wanted with a man was one of true and abiding love, like Marty had with Bob in Rosemary's SECRET BUTTERFLY SERIES™.

"Bob was Marty's steadfast lover, no matter what; no matter how many porn partners or affairs she had. Bob loved Marty through her love affairs with Carl, Fred, Big Ed, George and Bertie, Gwen, Maria, Dominick; all of those lovers. Bob loved Marty for who Marty was; for the woman she was, for that woman who loved him and who also lived her porn star life. Bob simply, totally, loved Marty. I told Brad that if we could have a love like that; an eternal reincarnating type of love that transcended many thousands of years and many hundreds of different corporeal bodies, then, and only then, would I want him as my lover.

John: "Well, did Brad agree to that? Did he divorce Cynthia?"

Ms. Sweets: "No, he could not agree. He could not stand the thought of staying loyal to me; and not ever being jealous of my other lovers. He could not comprehend the business aspects of porn; accepting me with other men, and loving me for being the real me. He wanted to be possessive and controlling. We talked it out. He needed a woman he could control. Brad went back to Cynthia. I have not seen him in years."

John: "Any regrets?"

Ms. Sweets: "No; none. A woman needs to know what's really inside a man's heart and head before she commits to a relationship with him. I wanted to be a porn star with many lovers and many affairs. I love having the relationships with many men. I love the picadilloes that spring out of my happenstance meetings on set and with my product sponsors and private members. I love all of it. I understand that all these relationships are centered on sexual pleasures; but I don't care. I totally love that aspect of it because I love having sex. Since Brad couldn't love me for who I was and the kind of life I wanted to have for myself; then, I knew he didn't really love me for me. He loved me for the woman he thought he could remake me into. It was better that we ended it."

John: "Well, have you found a man who loves you, for you; for this porn star life you're leading?"

Ms. Sweets: "Yes, I have. I have found that in Sam."

John: "But he's much older than you."

Ms. Sweets: "That doesn't matter. What matters is what is in his heart and his soul. He doesn't care that I'm a whore; that I have

*many other lovers and affairs; that I work my ass off;
practice tirelessly; and knock my brains out to create the
most sensational, mouthwatering porn that I can possibly
create. Sam loves me, for me. He appreciates me for my
dedication, relentless drive, and my work ethic. I know
that about Sam. I feel his love. It's absolute love. It's the
love that I need, for me."*

John: *"You're not just taking an old man for his money?"*

Ms.   *"Well, I am an unrepentant whore. But a lot of men have*
Sweets: *money. The real attraction for Sam is that he loves me for
me. He knows I'm a whore. He accepts that about me. He
knows money is part of our relationship. And he loves me
for that, too."*

John: *"For what?"*

Ms.   *"For taking him for half his fortune. He loves how my*
Sweets: *mind works. He loves the whore in me."*

John: *"How do you know that? I mean, what makes you so
sure?"*

Ms.   *"Well, it's a chemistry thing. It's what I feel inside. It's the*
Sweets: *same thing every woman feels inside herself when a man
holds her in his embrace and kisses her. She can tell by
how he kisses her whether he loves her for whom she is; for
all her failings and shortcomings, as well as her positive
attributes. She knows whether she's being loved for show,
or for sex, or for the real her that lives inside her soul.
Sam knows my soul, John. He knows I'm an incorrigible
whore. He knows I have fewer morals than a female ally
cat; yet he loves me unconditionally. He knows that I do
porn for a living. He knows that I have relationships with
many men. He knows that's just who I am; and he loves
me for me. He's not about changing me into someone I'm
not. He loves me just the way I am."*

John: *"Wow, Sweets, that's beautiful. Can you tell me something about your dedication to creating your exquisite pornography?"*

MSs
Sweets: *"Sure. Well, as you might imagine, there are thousands of expressions a girl can make with her face, her eyes, and her lips while she's seducing a man; or while she's performing fellatio; or fornicating. When you think about it, there are endless variations in the ways my lips kiss and the ways my tongue licks the heads of the penises I perform with; or the ways that I suck them and stroke them. If you'll carefully study my films, I think you'll discover that there are no two identical methods of seduction, fellatio, or fornication in my scenes.*

John: *"What do you like most about performing porn?"*

Ms.
Sweets: *"Everything. I love everything about my performances. I love the variety of things I can do with my partners; exploring each new penis and my new partner who comes with that penis; feeling that new penis inside me; knowing that I'm going to orgasm with it. I love the creativity challenge of performing at my most erotic best with each new partner and every penis. It's very exciting. It's my mind exploring all the different ways I can pleasure my partners; things I can do in our scenes to make them fall crazy into love with me. From my films, you'll see that no two partners receive the exact same sexual experience. That's part of the artistry of creating exceptional erotica.*

"I love the artistic aspect of performing porn. I love drawing my viewers into my performances; keeping them excited for me and anticipating what things I might do next. I love the challenge of continuously enticing my viewers to want more of me. I consider my performances to be beautiful works of creation art. And, John, that doesn't

even begin to address all the different scenes and scripts; the different inflections of my voice and voice tones; the different positions of my face, mouth, lips, breasts, vagina; the different paces of the action in each scene. I live for being in this world I'm in; this endless, ever-changing world of stimulating, pleasurable erotica.

"You see, John, while I'm performing, I imagine that there are men out there watching my film. I imagine that some little thing I do, some few frames of a scene; perhaps the way I impart my first kiss to a man's lips or his penis; or maybe by the way I rub his penis against my vagina before I guide its head to penetrate my outer lips; whatever it is that I'm doing with my partner, I imagine some men are fixating that scene in their minds.

"I'm imagining that their fixation will cause them to lust after me for weeks or months or years. And I love thinking that I'm having that effect on some men out there. And that motivates me to create more and more porn. I'm driven to imagine that, by performing in many hundreds of films, I'll cause many millions of men to fixate something from one of my scenes in their minds. And, once they have those images of me emblazoned into their minds, I know they'll want more of me. It's creating that elusiveness, that temptation and teasing and beckoning that I do in my scenes. It keeps my admirers coming back for more of me. And that results in sales. I'm also paid very well for creating my film performances and for performing my live porn shows; but those monies are a small part of my income. I don't even perform for the money anymore. I'm established now. I don't need the money. But I love performing porn so much that I'd continue creating porn even if I wasn't

paid. I guess I'm as addicted to performing it as some men are addicted to watching it."

John: *"You mean, like you're a nympho?"*

Ms. Sweets: *"I guess so. Yeah, I guess I've become a nympho. It's having what some girls call the itch, and knowing I have it. It's knowing how splendid; wonderfully marvelous a penis makes my vag and my entire body feel when it's inside me. I mean it's like millions of tiny butterfly fingers become sensitized and stimulated; and they send their sensational impulses and messages of delight and joy through my entire body.*

"So, when I see my partner's penis for the first time, I just go crazy inside myself. I can't wait to have it inside me. And I know I should do fellatio first; before the penis ejaculates its semen. So, that sequence is a bit of a challenge for me. I adore my partners' penises; but at the same time, I'm anxious to have their penises inside me. I know I need to stay focused on my fellatio. I know I must pace myself. And then there's the challenge of putting something original into every porn scene I perform.

"You see, there's this thing about exceptional pornography. It requires endless variety and a creative mind. And I deliver that. That's why my fans can't just have one of my films. That's why many fans buy hundreds of them. And that's why the films aren't enough for many of my Premium Service Members. They also need to see me regularity and make love with me often. Some see me once or twice weekly. They can't live without having sex with me. And, yes, many of them are married."

John: *"Do their wives know?"*

Ms. Sweets: *"Ha! I'm sure they do. Women know what their men are doing."*

John: "Did Pete's wife know?"

MS. Sweets: "Well, John, my dear love, that is a delicate question, since there is a murder trial going on. Let's just say, hypothetically, I would be surprised if she didn't know. Pete was seeing me practically every day. He became obsessed with me. He would lie with me for hours, performing oral sex with me; giving me orgasms. He loved me best while I was having an orgasm. For Pete, our love became more about him giving me my pleasures than him having his."

John: "Do you think he murdered his wife?"

Ms. Sweets: "Oh, there you go again. What is it about you men? Why are you all so concerned about wives? I don't like thinking about them. In my world, they're basically a nuisance factor. So, to answer your question: I don't know. Maybe he did murder her. Maybe he didn't."

John: "Do you feel sorry for his wife and kids?"

Ms. Sweets: "Am I supposed to feel sorry for them? Why do you care how I feel about them?"

John: "They were humans who were murdered. Their lives were cut short."

Ms. Sweets: "Well, it's unfortunate for them that they were murdered by someone. But I'm not sorry that Pete is free of them. He loves me. He didn't love them; at least he didn't love them like he loves me. And if he beats this murder rap, he'll be free of them and free to be with me whenever he can arrange times with my Service."

John: "That seems a little cold hearted."

Ms. Sweets: "John, darling, I'm a whore, remember?"

John: "Are you religious? Do you attend services? Ever feel guilty about the 'sinful' life you lead? Is this something that you and Sam have discussed?"

Ms. Sweets: *"Wow, John, that's a lot to unpack. No, I'm not religious. No, I don't attend services. No, I do not feel guilty about the life I lead. And I don't consider my life to be a sinful life in the first place. I consider my life to be an emancipated, free life; free of religious dogma. And yes, Sam and I have talked about this. He feels the same way I feel."*

John: *"So, what is Sam's take on religion?"*

Ms. Sweets: *"Well, like me, he thinks it's all hogwash. Sam can take apart every homily story in the scriptures and give the allegorical reasoning behind it. He's a great thinker and researcher that way."*

John: *"For instance. Can you give me one?"*

Ms. Sweets: *"Sure. Let me give you two. Sam says the Garden of Eden story was invented by males in the early tribes as part of their oral tradition. This began somewhere between twenty thousand years ago and six thousand years ago. Sam says there's no such place as a physical Garden of Eden. He claims that there was this multi millennial transition period from when the early tribes believed in prostitution worship. They regarded the woman's womb as the holy of holies. They held ceremonies which began with the appointed high tribal priests performing cunnilingus with the tribal prostitutes, to get them stimulated before they fornicated with all the other male members of the tribes.*

"There was no physical garden. The two rivers that came together into the garden were the females' fallopian tubes. The other two, incidental rivers that were sometimes flowing in the garden were the male and female urinary tracts, which sometimes leaked a little during the fornication ceremonies. This time period was when women began realizing that they could use certain herbs, ingested internally or a small parcel of an herb physically

placed inside their vaginas, which enabled them to have pleasurable sex without fear of getting pregnant. The Tree of Knowledge story was the prehistoric discovery version of our modern-day birth control pill. It was the realization that a woman can enjoy pleasures, without getting pregnant. So, the Garden of Eden is everywhere. It's inside every woman's pussy. There was no snake, no forbidden fruit, no tree of knowledge, and no God. That's all just homily hokum."

John: *"And the tribal women were okay with the fornication ceremonies?"*

Ms.   *"They more or less accepted them as necessary to keep
Sweets: the tribe united in purpose; having a common purpose and faith, if you will. The tradition of cunnilingus with the tribal prostitutes survives today in a modified form. When the Torah is removed from the arc at the beginning of Jewish worship services, it is paraded through the temple members. Members touch their prayer books to the Torah and then kiss their prayer books to symbolically declare that they have received the word of God. That practice survives from when early tribal members first kissed the vaginas of the tribal prostitutes before they fornicated with them; before their penises entered the prostitute's holy of holies.*

"Sam thinks those early tribes also tolerated polygamous relationships amongst tribal members. Women who felt stressed over watching their favorite male relationship fornicating with a tribal priestess prostitute were made to sit in the back of the gathering and were screened off by a curtain of tree branches. This 'women must sit behind a screen' tradition still exists in orthodox synagogues."

John: *"But how does Sam think original prostitution worship got started?"*

Ms.
Sweets: *"He thinks it began much like Rosemary described the explicit event in one of her books. One of the tribes brought down a mastodon. The hunters rejoiced in their success. They mocked the dead beast and exulted in their dominion over it. Humanity's first religious ceremony took place on the body of that beast. It makes sense."*

John: *"I see. You said you'd give me two allegories."*

Ms.
Sweets: *"Okay. Another of Sam's favorites is the Christian story of Salome and John the Baptist. Sam thinks the biblical version of what actually happened was to assert the primacy of Christianity over Paganism. But what Sam believes actually happened was the Pagan traditions triumphed. The world was not yet ready for Christianity. Sam thinks the decapitation happened. He thinks Salome fornicated directly in front of John the Baptist's eyes.*

"He thinks Salome's request to the king was to force the Baptist to stare at her whoring pagan vagina; observe semen flowing from it while she mocked him, much like the lesbian temptation scene from Rosemary's 'A WOMAN'S VOICS©' book. While the Baptist was forced to watch Salome's victorious, semen flowing, vagina, he came to realize that her immoral, ungodly, Pagan vagina was what the King chose to deify; not the abstract, unseeable God that he was promoting.

"It's the original story of the salesman who fails miserably. When the Baptist realized his failure, he pleaded for his life. He even groveled to Salome. But Salome did not want any new belief system challenging the supremacy of prostitution worship. She showed no mercy. She

demanded that the Baptist's head be severed from him and given to her as a symbolic trophy, in honor of her spectacular fornications."

John: *"And you believe Sam's interpretations of these historical events?"*

Ms. Sweets: *"Yes, absolutely I do. They make more sense to me than the biblical homilies."*

John: *"You mentioned Rosemary's books. You've read them?"*

Ms. Sweets: *"Yes. They connected with me. I couldn't stop reading once I started; couldn't put them down."*

John: *"I didn't know you were a reader."*

Ms. Sweets: *"Let me guess. You thought I was stupid because I do porn, right?"*

John: *"I didn't say that."*

Ms. Sweets: *"You didn't have to. But just so you know, lots of porn stars, like myself, are college educated and highly intelligent. We're just more open about our sexuality and less inhibited about having multiple relationships than most women."*

John: *"What drew you in? I mean to start you reading Rosemary's books."*

Ms. Sweets: *"Me. I saw myself in them. I felt the same feelings reading them that I feel in my real life. I could feel the loves I've felt; the men I've used; the men I've loved. I felt sympathy, rage, passion, disgust. Rosemary took my feelings all over the place. She's excellent at building up the suspense in a situation, like she did with Maria and her emancipation from her impossible mother; and like she did with Jen and her escape from her control freak mother; and how she brought the reader along in Sheila's story, getting her past her obsession with Pasqual and setting up the plot so she could see that Danny was the love she wanted all along. It's very clever plot design. I like that.*

"And I loved how Rosemary fitted her reincarnated characters' redemption themes to actual historical events. I mean, she had me right there, in Cleopatra's bedroom. I could really believe that I was Cleopatra; and, there I was fucking Caesar! How great is that! What porn star wouldn't want to know what it feels like to have that kind of power? And Susan with her billions of dollars of jewels: Building her story up to that sensational triumph! What porn star wouldn't like knowing how it feels to pull off a caper like that?"

John: *"You didn't feel revulsion?"*

Ms. Sweets: *"Only by David's character. What a despicable person. I couldn't imagine any man being that evil; that devious."*

John: *"But Susan scamming all those jewels and artwork? Didn't you feel repulsed by her character? Those jewels came from survivors of one of history's greatest atrocities. I mean, it's a little like: Okay, so the survivors got away with their lives; but Susan ended up with their wealth, so only part of them got away. She benefitted by their impoverishment. Doesn't that disgust you?"*

Ms. Sweets: *"John, you pitifully ignorant man. Don't you know me by now? I'm a lot like Susan and Marty and Sheila and Jen in Rosemary's books. They were whores who worshipped pleasure, money, and power. I'm a whore, too, remember? And you love me for who I am, don't you?"* Ms. Sweets kissed John's lips and smiled her eyes into his, as if that gesture made everything about her immorality all right.

John: *"Well, Frank, there you have some insights into Ms. Sweets' motive for becoming a porn star, and her way of thinking. Can you see that, for her, making love is a form of doing business? She may fall into love and out of love with many men. Can you see that she believes this is normal?"*

Frank: *"Yes, I do see that. But didn't it strike you as odd that her response to your question about the murders was evasive? She didn't actually address your question. Her response was classically narcissistic. She doesn't care about Marge and her kids. All she cares about is Pete's freedom from them. I guess that stems from her anti-religious belief system. It's almost as if she's glad they were murdered. I wonder whether she had a hand in their murders?"*

John: *"But how would that benefit her?"*

Frank: *"More time with Pete? Money, somehow?"*

John: *"Perhaps. But she had an ironclad alibi for her whereabouts when the murders took place. She was in bed with me."*

Frank: *"Yes, but she may have conspired with Pete, or urged him to kill them."*

John: *"No way. Your thinking has gone off the rails. Pete didn't do it."*

Frank: *"Right. That's not the Pete we know. I suppose Ms. Sweets just has a hard time thinking deeply about anything except her peccadillos. As she goes through life, her concerns are only about her pleasures, her loves and lovers, and her wealth."*

John: *"Absolutely true. The woman is focused."*

Frank: *"Yeah, focused. No moral compass. No human empathy. I used to think that porn stars led dual lives where they were sweetheart girl next door one day and secretly creating porn other days."*

John: "Maybe most are like that. But I think the highly successful ones are thinking about their porn and creating their porn pretty much full time."

Frank: "I wonder, does Ms. Sweets' mind ever stray from thoughts of sex and money?"

John: "Afraid not. At least not for long. That purposeful focus is what enables the most notorious porn stars to shed morality and loyalty and fidelity to any one man. It's what makes them so deliciously, immorally scrumptious. It's what makes men salivate to know them better; to copulate with them. They have that elusive, mysterious component about their personas. They defy the traditional view of how a woman is expected to behave. They represent a challenge to be tamed; but they cannot be tamed. Does understanding Ms. Sweets' focus help you see why porn stars have become so highly prized and compensated for their product endorsements; their roles in full, feature length films; their companionships as escorts and marital partners?"

Frank: "Marriage partners while still performing their porn?"

John: "Especially while they are still performing their porn. Their porn craft makes them that much more desirable in the eyes of many alpha males. It's an ego thing to have a notorious porn star on your arm. Alpha males know that inferior males cannot afford or sufficiently pleasure them."

Frank: "Oh, yes, I see that. The trophy wife aspect of marriage."

John: "Exactly. And that returns our focus to the topic of Ms. Sweets. You should know that Sam proclaimed Ms. Sweets as his 'Chosen.' That's not a small thing."

Frank: "You mean he decided to persuade her to convert to Judaism and become a Jew, like him?"

John: *"No, Frank. Jews don't proselytize; not that kind of chosen; not one of God's people; no, Sam meant that Ms. Sweets should become one of 'his' people; a fellow human being that he personally favors. And that is huge for Ms. Sweets. In Sam's world, that makes her more important than God. Sam decided to take to her in; give her his financial support; finance her movies; and love her as both a father figure and a lover. He wants to help her explode onto the mainstream film world and make her the dominant female fixture in the public mind."*

Frank: *"Like becoming her Sugar Daddy?"*

John: *"It's something like that; but it's more like being an invisible hand that helps her. You see, Frank, as much as Sam loves porn, he views the entire porn industry as a poor stepchild to the big screen blockbuster films that he envisions for the future. He calls today's porn films: 'Porn Skits,' connoting that they are a kind of bargain-basement, low-priced fare where young girls hope to get discovered. It's a good venue for young girls who are naturally promiscuous; for adventuresome girls who are willing to be fondled and penetrated as a means for showing off their acting potentials. Porn is a logical entertainment industry stepping stone for many girls to advance themselves to bigger roles. It's analogous to a young baseball player deciding to play for a double A minor league team while hoping to get a shot at playing for a major league team."*

Frank: *"Or like the practice squad in NFL football?"*

CHAPTER SIX

FROM RELIGION TO HUMANISM

John: *"Yeah, something like that. Anyway, Sam has two overriding goals in mind. He wants to take pornography mainstream and produce full, feature length film series'; sagas, long running serial shows that tell meaningful stories which include credible, breathtaking explicit erotica seduction scenes."*

Frank: *"You mean a series that is X rated?"*

John: *"Yes, that's what Sam wants to produce. He believes society is ready for it; in the spirit of full transparency; and ready to move beyond R ratings to X ratings as standard fare. He's studied the data trends for porn viewership. I have to agree with him. We're seeing a tidal wave. Who is to say he isn't right? I mean, who doesn't want to see the recreations of what actually happened in Cleopatra's bedroom between her and Caesar and between her and Marc Anthony? Who doesn't want to see all the erotic things that Salame did to earn herself the head of John the Baptist? Who doesn't want the unabridged version of the explicit things that Sarah did with Egypt's Pharoah and his sons? Sam opines that the public is craving to see those things and understand them. They want full transparency and Sam intends to give it to them. He wants to be in the forefront of film producers who deliver a new, higher level, explicit entertainment product."*

Frank: *"And his second goal?"*

John: *"He wants to lift Ms. Sweets out of 'Double A' baseball and place her in the Majors. Sam feels driven about this. He adores the girl next door innocence of Ms. Sweets. He empathizes with her desire to continue producing the world's most gorgeous pornography; and he wants the entire world to lie down before her and worship her as the most desired, most loved, film actress of all time; even more adored than Elizabeth Taylor, Betty Davis, or Marilyn Monroe were in their times.*

"I know Sam. He intends to make Ms. Sweets into a goddess. And he will succeed. He always does. He will do whatever it takes to ensconce her as the most notorious porn goddess in all of history. And I can see why. She brings unique qualities to her porn craft. For example, in her films you always hear her mirthful giggle and you perceive how she simply assumes that every man's cock belongs to her; how all cocks are presented to her for her enjoyment.

"She enthusiastically lavishes her loving slobber upon her partners' cocks and their testicle sacs; demonstrably proving that she is thoroughly enjoying herself. She performs her craft without the slightest hesitation or sense of self-consciousness. And she's so beautifully natural about it. She's every man's dream girl; and she's living right next door, just one mouse click away. And her eyes and smiles and body language convey that she's completely at home in her own skin; loving herself; feeling the rapture of her

calling, while performing her porn. Sam loves displaying her passion for her porn craft."

Frank: *"She thinks even married men's cocks belong to her, doesn't she?"*

John: *"Yes, Frank; especially married men's cocks. She loves the game of 'Take Away.' She's mentally wired a lot like the Marty character in Rosemary's books. She's a predator who takes what she wants without any feelings of guilt or remorse; a true vamp. In one of Rosemary's book segments, Marty intentionally sets out to destroy a Muslim woman's marriage. I've never read anything more sinfully salacious. Now, every time I watch one of Ms. Sweets' films, I cannot help but wonder how many married men's cocks she has enjoyed fucking; how many marriages she's upended? I wonder how many men have felt sinfully blessed while entering her wonderous honey pot?*

"Thinking about her in that prurient way becomes an obsession; like a compulsion to pay homage to evil. But I can't help myself. I want her. And I'm willing to accept her sinfulness as the price of having her. I wonder when it will be that I am finally with her again; when I can succumb to her charms again? And when will I make that call; join her premium service; go to her; make love with her? I know what this makes you think of me, Frank. But I can't help it. I must see her. I believe that day when I can ejaculate my semen into her again will be the most wonderous day of my life. It will be my surrender day."

Frank: *"You said 'again.' You did her?"*

John: *"Yes. I described it to you. I couldn't help myself. I had to."*

Frank: *"I never knew porn stars could effect a man that way."*

John: *"They can, Frank. They are having a profound effect on many men; and they are having it on women, too. They are modern-day missionaries. They are changing the attitudes and morality of the world; introducing a new way of understanding what is right and wrong. I think they are showing us a better way to think about human relationships and acceptance. It's a beautiful, wonderful thing. Porn stars are humanity's blessing."*

Frank: *"You believe that?"*

John: *"Yes, absolutely I do; totally."*

Frank: *"And Mandy? Was Ms. Sweets even more wondrous than Mandy on your wedding night?"*

John: *"Yes, much better. Incomparably better; that's the honest truth of it. I know it's all lust based. But I couldn't help myself. Something happened in my mind. It was my release from shame; my defiance of guilt and inhibition. It was indescribably beautiful; so wonderous; so free from cares. I can't explain it. Maybe it was Ms. Sweets' experience. Whatever it was, Ms. Sweets gave me a spiritual awakening. I knew I was surrendering my soul to a porn star; and I very much wanted to do that. That's exactly what I wanted to do because I knew I would feel released from my burdens when I did.*

"I accepted a truth about my honest needs. I knew I was finally being honest with myself; and that was a beautiful thing. I accepted the fact that I needed Ms. Sweets. I still need her. So, I know I'll make that call again. I am a mere mortal man. I cannot resist her. Call it the Ms. Sweets effect; whatever you want to make of it. I don't care. I only know that she took control of my limbic mind and set it free. I don't want to resist her. I want to embrace her and love her. I want that sense of freedom she gives me. Like many other men, I also love her, emotionally. I mean that. Despite being married, I honestly love Ms.

Sweets. I must have her. I know I cannot marry her, like Sam will do. I must pay to be with her. But, nevertheless, I love her. I'm hopeless."

Frank: *"Hopeless like Pete was?"*

John: *"Yes, I think so. When she's kissing one of her porn partners with her gorgeous long legs spread, welcoming his fingers inside her, stimulating her, I cannot help but obsessing over how many cocks have been inside her ravenous vagina; how many have ejaculated their huge volumes of semen inside her glorious pussy. I desperately long to join them, Frank. I must join them. I want to kiss her and hold her. I want to fuck her. I need to fuck her. I must fuck her. I'll never be at peace with myself until I do. Maybe for no sane, understandable reason, I'm smitten; mesmerized; compelled to honor her immorality; even sanctify it.*

"I desperately desire to pay my manly tribute to her spectacular whoring, again and again. I'm compelled to honor her insatiable, cock craving vagina with my ejaculations. In all my life, never have I felt such urges; such compulsions to fuck any other woman. Her pornography has captured my soul and brought this yearning upon me. I must become one of her lovers. I feel my soul being drawn into her soul; obsessing over her, like Pete must have felt. I'm ready to do anything; give anything to have her. But like you, I could never kill my wife over a piece of ass. I could never do that. And I don't think Pete killed Marge."

Frank: *"I don't think he killed her either. We'll be there at his trial for him. And we'll finance his appeal if he loses. And we'll hire a good private eye to figure out who really killed Marge and the kids. But you mentioned Sam wanting to produce a series. You said he wants Ms. Sweets to play the starring role in this? Can you tell me about it?"*

John: "Sure. Like I said, it's going to be based on a saga, the book series called 'THE SECRET BUTTERFLY SERIES ™'. It was written by Rosemary Ness Bitner, that's the pen name for Sam's cousin. I'm sure Sam and his cousin have a deal where Sam finances the work for a piece of the Series book sales and film rights."

Frank: "But what is the series about?"

John: "Transition. It's about transition of society from religious ordering to secular humanism; about the triumph of socialism, hedonism, and promiscuous immorality; about organized male hierarchical religions taking a back seat to progress and pleasure; equality of woman; interracial romance and sex; the whole ball of wax. It's a sensitive treatment about the permutations of human behaviors and changes in morality that flow from this transition. It examines the effects of pornography on the lives of all the people that pornography touches and the changes that pornography has historically brought about in our social cultures.

"It begins with the story of a young girl named Marty. Her mother abandoned her to an East Coast boarding school. She becomes the world's most notorious femme fatale; porn star extraordinaire; accomplished in business and all the ways of the world."

Frank: "And Sam wants Ms. Sweets to play the role of Marty, right?"

John: "Bingo! Well, this Marty reconciles herself to the fact that her mother doesn't love her. She becomes promiscuous. There are episodes in the Series where Marty seduces boys and men, including her geometry teacher. She also takes the prize alpha male away from his socialite girlfriend. While discovering her sexuality, she does pussy kiss-kiss *with her girlfriend; and attracts devoted male lovers. Eventually, she's working in an investment firm where she trades sex for sales. She gets it on with a top salesman and she wants him all to herself. So, she figures out a way to murder his wife. It's pure genius; a perfectly executed murder.*

"Later, she discovers true love with Bob. She pries him away from his first love, Barbara. Of course, she does. She's the consummate seductress. Barbara has no chance. But Marty is a complex character; a nympho. Bob is not enough for her. She also has a special relationship with the Firm's owner, David. He's a neurotic deviant with side deals in nefarious dealings with a drug cartel. Marty's special, twisted relationship with David has Marty committing several delicious, romance-filled seductions and many murders."

Frank: *"She's a serial killer?"*

John: *"Enabled by David, yes."*

Frank: *"Sounds titillating and a bit macabre."*

John: *"Very titillating and scary macabre; also, deeply psycho probing and provocative. Let's just say that Marty is a victim who discovered shocking and deviant ways to thrive in her victimhood. And David is masterful at manipulating the situation; creating innovative ways of keeping Marty tied to him. Right and wrong gets blurred and inverted. And there's recovery to reality, which refreshes you. Sometimes the horror aspects of the saga stand up the hairs on the back of your neck. It thoughtfully treats controversial subjects in ways that capture the honest passion on both sides of the issues.*

"It touches on incest, abortion, antisemitism, racism, greed, lust, passion, manipulations, jealousies; even

explores the justifiable rationale for committing murder to advance the cause of human liberation. Honestly, Frank, in some places it makes you believe that a woman should feel no more guilt over having an abortion than she has over eating a potato chip; like it's perfectly normal. It reveals the disguised forms of good and evil. It deeply probes the role of religion in the human psyche; makes you question religion's role and come to grips with it and its effect on others as well as yourself."

Frank: *"It's allegorical?"*

John: *"Yes, definitely. The main character, Marty, has an extraordinary persona. She's the living antidote to religion and morality. She's also an unapologetic nympho who has flashbacks to her previous lives. The book has scenes where Marty recalls her lives as Asherah; Astarte; Athena; Aphrodite; two different tribal goddesses during Pagan worship times; Salome; Bathsheba; Sara; Eve; and Isabella. She even portrays Mary, as the Madonna of the Christ during her spiritual insemination scene; and, later, as Mary Magdalene, Christ's mistress, she performs the ultimate sacrilege at the foot of the cross, in full view of her dying, crucified lover. That scene takes your breath away. It's astounding; the ultimate reveal about the natural volatility of human behavior; how the mind can flip from rational control to limbic surrender, depending upon the circumstances. It explains why people often cannot control their behaviors.*

"The scene removes the viewers' mental focus from the pains and travails of religious beliefs to the joys and uninhibited pleasures of secular hedonism. A switch flips from morality to immorality. It's like a glorious dawn breaking. The film becomes not about the Christ, but about the

pleasures of a glorious, shamelessly profligate, deliciously immoral whore. Ms. Sweets is the perfect choice to play Marty's role as the reversionary Mary Magdalene here. It's like you can feel the Christ come and go from the world and her life. And you're left wondering whether his presence left a lasting effect on her, or merely a temporary one. Humanity still wrestles with that. I promise you: You will love Mary Magdalene and empathize with her more than you ever have before. Rosemary portrays her as a saint with insatiable human needs.

"I also promise you: The Series will heat you up; excite you; give you exhilarating mood swings; lift you up; have you gripping your seat in suspense; and make you feel good about being an imperfect human being. In film, it promises to be a breathtaking extravaganza of dramatic intrigue, emotionally charged acting, scorching hot passion, and spectacular eroticism.

Frank:	*"Sounds like the Series has a lot of seduction scenes."*
John:	*"Yes, and knowing Sam like I do, their filming will all be spectacularly and elegantly done. And Ms. Sweets will be showcased in every scene to be stunningly gorgeous. She's perfect for the roles. She's craven-crazed; obsessed with performing mesmerizing, exquisite erotica while creating her porn. Porn exhilarates her. She imagines she's lavishing her eroticism upon the minds behind the cameras. You can just feel how enthralled she becomes while delighting her penises and releasing her orgasms. You'll feel like you are there with her; becoming one with her.*

"I swear, Frank, the scenes with Marty and with Susan and their male partners will take your breath away. It's how Rosemary explains the happenings in the human mind while people experience lovemaking. She smoothly

transitions us from our frontal lobe cortex thinking, like we have with our wives, to amygdala induced limbic thinking, like I've experienced with Ms. Sweets. It's surrender to sin, Frank. It's embracing the wonders of it. And Rosemary connects you with the woman's feelings by relating what's happening between the clitoris and the penis and lovers' minds, while loving partners orgasm together. You'll feel the same sacred phenomena that Pagans experienced while practicing prostitution worship. It's healthy and exhilarating; and it returns us to our natural human roots through pornography. Porn stars are reintroducing limbic connectivity into our modern culture as a living, humanistic art form. It's taking root and becoming accepted and adored.

"Rosemary probes the mind set of an accomplished porn star seductress; explains how she slips into her moods while tantalizing her beaus. The Series books also showcase four orgy scenes, two of them with extremely well-endowed black partners. The author captures the thoughts of a porn star while performing with multiple lovers of different races. It's much more loving and romantic than you might imagine. You'll appreciate Marty's feelings.

"Let me explain. It's one thing to have sex with a woman, Frank. But try imagining that you are having sex with a porn star. Then imagine falling in love with her. Then go one step further. You appreciate that she's a nympho. Now, imagine that you become emotively attached to her libido. What I mean is: You feel intense empathetic love for her because you can empathize with how much she's loving her orgasms with her different porn partners. Rosemary's books take your mind into those deep, dark, human defining places. They take you

into deeper levels of romance; beyond passion and lust; beyond love; onward into eternity; into feelings of holiness. You'll adore Rosemary's characters. You'll even obsess over them.

"Then, when you finally do make love with Ms. Sweets, you'll find yourself encouraging her to give you all the romantic eroticism from your shared experience that she possibly can. You'll want to experience with her what's going through her mind; how she manages to forget everything else while she and you share this immoral, eternalizing bond. All of that will happen for you, Frank. Ms. Sweets is a sensational porn star. She will create those eternal feelings within you. You'll see. You'll love her. I promise."

Frank: *"Experience what goes through her mind, you say. Tell me, John, what do you think goes through her mind during the shared experience?"*

John: *"It could be any of a hundred different things, like Rosemary explores with her books."*

Frank: *"Well, take me down just one rabbit hole. Could you do that much for me, please? Tell me what is going through Ms. Sweets' mind while she's seducing a married man for the first time."*

John: *"Okay. Well, I'm not sure. I can only relate it to the Marty character in Rosemary's books. Marty experienced a sort of triumph during her seductions of married men. She even had a neckless chain filled with wedding rings of those men. It was a psychic thing for her."*

Frank: *"A triumph?"*

John: *"Yeah, she thought of it as a victory over the forces of control, the religious forces. It was a moment of triumph for her; like a conversion ceremony in religion, complete with a ritual bath; or like a baptism of someone into a new kind of faith."*

Frank: *"Conversion? Baptism?"*

John: *"Yeah. Removing those men, or rather saving them and their souls from religious dogma and welcoming them into the new, accepting world of humanism."*

Frank: *"You mean accepting prostitution, pornography, and Paganism? You mean seeing those dystopian things as normal, acceptable things in everyday society?"*

John: *"Yes, absolutely; embracing the shift in morality to our newly enlightened immoral world, which is really the old immoral world; which was the perfectly moral, normal world of twelve thousand to six thousand years ago, before the religions got control of humanity and fucked everything up. Those early Pagans believed they were participating in a worship service. We are also believing that; only we call it pornography. Porn is actually a new, reconstituted form of an old religion. At least Sam thinks so."*

Frank: *"And you agree?"*

John: *"I do. Wait until you've been with Ms. Sweets. You'll also become a believer."*

Frank: *"Okay, I'll see her. So, you're saying she will change the way my mind perceives moral rights and wrongs. Am I getting this? And Sam thinks Ms. Sweets can personify some of the characters in Rosemary's books. Am I getting this?"*

John: *"Yes. It's not about love or even about lust. There's all that, for sure. And there's romance, too. Lots of emotive romance. But it's really about a change in your belief system; about accepting our new dystopian world; about opening you up to accepting women's sexuality; freeing them from religious bondage and loving them for their freedom. The books have many examples; many situations with many nuanced happenings; many techniques used to facilitate the belief conversions; much eroticism; but yes.*

"And Ms. Sweets seems like the perfect natural for many of the scenes. Sam told me she caught his eye by the way she touches her partners. Sam loves how Ms. Sweets thrills to perform her erotic touchings, especially during her orgy scenes. He remarked that she seems to know Rosemary's scenes like she's read the books. He wants every foreplay portion of the books' orgy scenes to be all-hands-on Ms. Sweets' body affairs.

"But Sam insists that the actual fellatio and fornication segments will be produced sequentially, showing Ms. Sweets igniting the limbic passions of each individual partner; flooding him with her passion; drowning his inhibitions and moral convictions; and seducing him to ejaculation. Sam intends to stretch the filming timetable to ensure that Ms. Sweets will be her winsome, freshest, erotic best with every partner."

Frank: *"That may take days!"*

John: *"Sam knows. He doesn't care what it costs. He'll leave it to the film director to splice the scenes to make each orgy a continuous scene. The important thing to Sam is that Ms. Sweets becomes firmly established in the minds of viewers as the most delectable, elegant, irresistibly desirable goddess of sex and seduction the world has ever seen.*

"This video saga will have the most memorable, most exquisite porn scenes ever produced. And Ms. Sweets will be memorialized as the world's most glorious, promiscuous, shamelessly wanton, incorrigible femme in all of

human history. Sam will showcase her 'It' factor. I can tell, Sam has a thing for this woman. He's smitten and in love. I know Sam. He'll make her famous. And she'll become one of the world's wealthiest women."

Frank: *"All because Sam loves her porn; because of the way she seduces and fucks her porn partners has ignited Sam's limbic fires?"*

John: *"Yes. I've never known Sam to become this obsessed over any other woman. He has to have her. He has to exalt her. In Sam's mind, Ms. Sweets has displaced God."*

Frank: *"That' no small thing. Sam must believe that porn is the future of our culture. He must believe that porn is our new religion."*

John: *"He does. He's a visionary. He thinks the future belongs to women who excel in intimate artistry. Porn stars open our eyes to the pleasures that enlightened societies have historically embraced. It's a phenomenon that happens when societies, like the Babylonians, the Romans, and the Nazis, mature and attained their pinnacles of power. That's when debauchery flourished. Women who exceled at erotica during these times were revered and adored. Girls who grow up today, learning to become good girl scouts, selling their girl scout cookies and training to become compliant housewives and ordinary workers will simply be left behind."*

Frank: *"Why eighteen films? "Why so many?"*

John: *"Because the Secret Butterfly Series™ is a saga replete with many stories, plots, twists, and permutations. For example, Marty's mother, Susan, also to possibly be played by Ms. Sweets, is a seductress in her own right. She seduces Marvin, the Firm's original founder. Without giving away any of the plots, I must tell you that much of the Series touches on real historic happenings. A man similar to Rosemary's Marvin's character existed in real life. He set up the escape lines to get Jews out of Nazi Germany in exchange for a fabulous hoard of jewels. He also set up the rat lines with Colonel Juan Peron to help Nazis flee the allies and escape to Argentina, also in exchange for priceless artworks and billions of dollars' worth of precious jewels. Sam told me that the Series stories about the Jewish escape lines and the Nazi rat lines are representative of real-life stories; that the jewels and artworks removed from Nazi Germany were real. Sam and his cousin Rosemary swear they have seen the actual jewels and know where they are hidden. Marvin's real-life counterpart secreted away many billions of dollars' worth of stolen Jewish art and relics; and several thousand pieces of priceless art and artifacts.*

"Marvin and Susan's real-life counterparts fornicated often in front of those priceless works of art; then they toasted champaign to themselves and their successful operations. They were beyond sacrilegious and ribald. They were shameless, uninhibited, depraved pleasure seekers, celebrating their own charms and wits, pulling off history's greatest caper. And they've never paid a dime of taxes on any of it! Their jewel hoard is easily worth over one hundred billion dollars in today's dollars. In one of the Series' scenes, Susan, Marvin's mistress, fornicates on pillows, atop over a hundred billion dollars' worth of diamonds, rubies, and emeralds. She and Marvin defile his faith and his marriage; personifying greed, lust, and wrath.

"Susan's seduction scenes are the crux of the greed thread which runs through the Series. Her character

pioneers humanity's current chapter, where it abandons its religious adherences to embrace hedonistic secularism. And who, today, can cast blame upon Marvin and Susan, or those who suffered the horrors of the Nazi's? After the holocaust and the horrors that the world went through, it's no wonder many stopped believing in God. Susan and Marvin were among the post world wars' first dedicated non-believers. They decided to only believe in themselves. They became secular humanists; hedonists; human jackals, cleverly preying upon the helpless. And they did extremely well.

"But Susan's character is a classic romantic. She loves romance and loves being in love. Marvin's character does several erotic scenes with her. And Susan performs three erotic scenes with her other lovers, including one threesome. In that scene, Marvin wears a hand-crafted wedding ring, designed to represent the flag of Israel. There's a seminal moment where Marvin, a revered pillar of the Jewish community, forsakes his wife, passionately kisses Susan, and succumbs to her irresistible charms. Love overtakes both of them. Susan ignites Marvin's limbic zone, prompting him to symbolically surrender his faith, his Zionism, and his soul.

"Her secular immorality ultimately absorbs Marvin's psyche; takes control of it and dominates him. Role reversals take place during an explicit erotic exchange. Proud, unshakable Marvin loses his will to resist. He capitulates to Susan. From then on, Marvin's mind and soul belong to her. The entire purpose of Marvin's life and the efforts of his firm turn towards serving Susan: bringing her more lovers and showering her with unfathomable wealth."

Frank: *"Sounds like this series is laced with antisemitism."*

John: *"Perhaps bigots could take it that way; but that would be an incorrect read. It's just as anti-Christian and anti-Islam as it is anti-Semitic. The Series' stories actually aren't anti-anything. They just make you question what you believe and present an alternative. They start out with the character developments of Marvin, Susan, and her daughter, Marty. Marvin is a prominent Jew who hates his situation. Essentially, he's living a lie. Susan is the gorgeous schlepp victim of Marvin's domineering wife, Eloweiss. Unlike Marvin, Susan doesn't self-loath; but she does hate her situation. It depresses her and drives her to promiscuity. She recognizes her parents as close-minded schmucks. When Marvin and Susan discover each other: Vahvoom! Sparks fly. They create their own world. And they visit their creation upon the rest of the world; gleefully devouring that morality-based world like it's their personal oyster."*

Frank: *"They turn the world's misfortunes into their personal gain, right? And they fuck a lot?"*

John: *"Right. And oh, hell yeah! Like minks! Very explicit, breathtaking romantic eros. Like pillow talk like you've never heard before. They even have their offices modified to facilitate their pleasuring. That's why the films will be perfect for Ms. Sweets. The characters logically question the rational for morality. And they come up empty.*

"Marvin tosses away conformity and morality. He becomes so enamored with Susan that he has his friend, Ep, film their revelries. Alas, Marvin's wife, Eloweiss, discovers Marvin's photographs and films. She sees that Marvin has led a debauched other life with Susan. She writes a letter which expresses things I cannot mention here. Eloweiss and her family are pillars of the Jewish

community. Marvin has hell to pay. The mystery surrounding the jewels and the precious art works then goes deeply underground. But it lives on into the present day, for real. Only two people living today know where the jewels and art works are securely hidden. But thus far, they aren't telling.

"Marvin's psychopathic son, David, injects a twisted psychological element to the Series. David's character is the ultimate control freak. He graduates from his childhood days of pulling wings off flies to become a serial killer, corporate prankster, financial bully, murderer, and avowed anti-black racist. His criminal antics spawn the Firm's new business venues of prostitution, drug dealing, child trafficking, illicit gambling schemes, money laundering, murders, and body disposal operations. His twisted mind holds imaginary conversations with Dolly, his black sheep, and Don.

"Don is David's nickname for Adonai, God of the Hebrews. David fantasizes himself in dogged pursuit of his ultimate revenge goal. He intends to lead an army of tiny hat Jew warriors. They set out to retake the vast Russian Steppes that were stolen from his ancestors by the Tzar's pogroms. He frequently imagines himself leading a charge of thousands of Jews who storm into Russia, driving armored Cadillacs, modified for combat with the Russian army. He's also the self-appointed disaster warning service for his city. He's a total psycho. His antics are so insane, they're hilarious."

Frank: *"Sounds like quite a bizarre fellow."*

John: *"He is. David is the byproduct of his father Marvin's attempt to flee his patriarchal heritage, which is telescoped and personified into the family's ancestral chair. Marvin wrestles with the significance of the chair and ultimately gives the chair and all its associated burdens to David. Of course, David cannot cope with the weightiness of tradition. He holds everything and everyone associated with his lineage in contempt. David appreciates nothing. David respects nothing. His misanthropy sends him on his journey into psychopathy. His hatred of all things human causes him to meet out vengeance on his firm's executives, employees, and clients. Ultimately, his psyche takes him still lower. He plumbs the deepest depths of depravity until, at last, he discovers the loves of his life; his relatable soulmates—the insects. He and his trusted fetus in a formaldehyde jar confidant become enthralled spectators at the insects' gladiator games. Yes, David does many unimaginable things that open vistas far beyond nasty and creepy. Yet, author Rosemary somehow makes him understandably palatable by infusing him with heaping helpings of disarming patrician charm. You'll empathize with David. You'll love him and you will simultaneously hate him."*

Frank: *"Her books are character studies, then?"*

John: *"Definitely. And more than that, they are examinations of relationships; the twists and turns in human interactions that reveal the bedrock of each character. David and Marty, for example, are paired like two binary stars. They psychically, mutually depend upon each other while their independent sociopathic lives continuously orbit each other. It's a mutually reinforcing dynamic that ensures both characters stay committed to their ungodly partnership. It's a character study of evil as well as a study of personas.*

"And both characters are purposeful serial murderers. Marty's murders are driven by her psychological need

to recreate her childhood. Rosemary builds empathy for Marty's character through childhood scenes where the reader sees her transformative departure from innocence. As a reader, you might think that, surely, something or someone will intervene to stop Marty's fall. But no one does. Not her shrinks; not her teachers; not her classmates; and least of all, her mother.

"David's motive for his murders is different. It is fueled by his all-consuming hatreds. In that sense, they are less personal murders than Marty's murders. David despises other Jews, especially his parents. But David also hates Christians, Muslims; and he reserves a special contempt for a certain black man. In this chilling horrific segment, Rosemary reveals David's true character. His is one of the most fascinating characters you'll ever encounter. Certainly, he is bizarre. Bizarre in his habits; his manipulations of others; and in his dealings with the demons that reside in his mind, David enables his behaviors by immersing himself in a delusional psychic bubble of his own creation.

"And when a certain black man unwittingly pricks David's bubble image of himself, David retaliates in the most despicable, heinous way. The infinite dimensions of David's hatreds are revealed. They are irrational and chilling; and despite all intrusions of logic, David clings tightly to them. He needs his hatreds. Hate is his ultimate retreat and refuge from the outside world. Tellingly, and most of all, David hates himself. He conceals his self-loathing well until he can no longer contain it. It erupts in his tearful confession. His true feelings about himself escape in his excursions with Bob. Rosemary steadily builds readers' revulsion for her David character; yet, when his character

reveals its true self in his stunning climax confession, she makes his unacceptable hatreds understandable; at least from David's perspective. His is a deeply, psychically wounded persona.

"Like Marty, David was also neglected as a child. And, like Marty, he was raised in an environment that taught him to believe he was different from other people. Marty rebelled. She used promiscuity to break free of her inferiority cocoon. David did not rebel. He succumbed to teachings that taught him to believe he was superior to others; so much so that he developed contempt and hatred towards his fellow humans, and himself. His cocoon gripped him tighter.

"An unspoken, vaguely mysterious bond develops between our two dysfunctional Marty and David characters. They initiatively understand that they need each other to perform many of their murders. And that is where Rosemary's plot thickens. David has a key advantage. He has a deep understanding of their bond and he uses it to deceive and ensnare Marty. Marty dimly senses that the bond exists, but she can't understand why it holds her so closely to David. She even mistakes it for mutual sexual attraction. During two chilling horror segments, Rosemary explains how the bond becomes the driving force behind our characters' unconscionable murders. Marty and David are captives to their mutual bond. Much like binary stars, they feel an empathetic need to always be near each other; and to continue their mutual dependency.

"David's Firm is merely a front for his criminal enterprises. Marty naturally becomes David's model employee. He loves her freedom from inhibition and admires her

willingness to reject morality in order to become success-ful. After molding the firm to accommodate her exceptional seduction talents, David champions Marty's goal of becoming the world's most notorious porn star.

"Stronger together, neither character can escape their perverse mutual attraction bond. It holds them in, drawing them ever closer to each other. Somehow it is stronger than their loves for others; and it grows ever stronger with the passage of time. Their fabulous mutual success and massive illicit wealth fates them to live as dependent slaves to their ungodly, inseparable relationship, despite both of them secretly desiring to escape from it."

Frank: *"Sounds a bit heavy and terrifying. Must I swallow a glass of scotch while reading her books? Why do I feel like I'll need to hold onto something?"*

John: *"Unless you are easily emotionally unstuck, I think you'll be okay, Frank. They're well written. They're not 'Ah ha, gotcha' kind of tales. There is some of that, but mostly, it is chock-a-block filled with breathtaking romances, intrigue, shocking murders, hilarity, insanity, and salacious seduction scenes. It's empathetic and zany; a journey into humanity's bedrock best and worst behaviors. You'll find yourself wondering if there really are people whose minds work in such twisted ways. Trust me, Frank, there are. Rosemary found them. She brings them to you.*

"The Series will help you identify them. You'll love how Rosemary takes your mind into the minds and thoughts of her characters. It's exceptional work; intriguing and provocative; filled with intertwining love stories and drama. It will turn your mind upside down and inside out; take you to the highest heights of human benevolence; and plunge you into bottomless dark places;

into the deepest, most debauched, depraved abysmal recesses of base human behavior. Sam thinks it's masterful literature."

Frank: *"Not crap?"*

John: *"No, Frank, not crap. I'm not saying you can't jerk off to it. Maybe you could. It's that vivid; that poignant in places. You'll recognize Marty's character in Ms. Sweets. Rosemary brings the mental image of Ms. Sweets right onto your lap. She has you kissing and hugging her while she's joyfully fucking your brains out."*

Frank: *"So, it's base?"*

John: *"No, Frank, it isn't. It's the eye opener to overlapping worlds that few people even know exists. That's the genius of it. There are many happenings in the Series. There's the theme of seductresses taking control of men and their businesses. There's reincarnation themes, where the main characters pass away and become reborn into different times and settings. And there is this mentally disturbed chick, Marty. Marty's voices live within her troubled mind. They accompany her behaviors while she performs her seductions and murders. Yet, she's this thoroughly adorable character. You'll empathize with her responses to her inner voices. She'll melt your heart. You'll love her. She'll make you question all your beliefs. She'll even make you believe that her murders are good, necessary, curative therapy for her mental health. You'll find yourself loving Marty more and more, especially after she murders certain characters who try to use her."*

Frank: *"It's a woman empowerment thing?"*

John: *"Definitely. You'll find yourself absolving women who act up and take control. You'll see the world as they see it. Freedom of choice, for example, takes on a whole different perspective when you stand in a woman's shoes. The Series gives the abortion dilemma robust treatment in four different scenes; all of which are brim-filled with unique situational perspectives and emotion. The Series' readers and film goers will fall in love with the characters. They'll love them and empathize with their conflicts, especially Rosemary's Susan and Marty characters; but also, Maria, Sheila, Cecilia, Lotus, Sandra, Joanne, Linda, and Jen. I cried when I read some of their stories. I couldn't help it; they were that romantic and realistic. I felt emotive love for all of them. You'll see. You'll meet them in the Series and you'll understand them. You'll become acutely aware of their character traits and find yourself seeking a relationship with women you meet who have feelings just like theirs."*

Frank: *"You mean with prostitutes?"*

John: *"No, Frank. I mean the hidden traits and the disguised attributes detectable in any woman whom you'd never suspect of having one ounce of prurient blood in her veins. But many women do possess those traits. Once you understand the characters of Maria, Sheila, Connie, Joanne, Linda, Sandra, Pattie, Jen, and Lotus Lulabelle Wong, you will never look at butterflies the same way again."*

Frank: *"Butterflies?"*

John: *"Yeah Frank, butterflies. The reincarnated characters of Marty carry the butterflies' spirits. They relate with and interplay with humans' spirits in the spiritual realm. Butterflies do their metamorphosis thing for a very special reason. That's how they relate to us humans, Frank. Read and learn."*

Frank: *"Okay, But how does Sam expect Ms. Sweets to play all these different characters?"*

John: *"Well, he'll need to get additional porn stars for the roles of Lotus, Joanne, Linda, Sandra, Pattie, and a few others that I haven't even mentioned. I'm not a movie producer or director person. But I think the main roles of Susan, Marty, Sheila, Cecilia, and Connie could all be played by Ms. Sweets. And that should not be a problem because those characters come into the Series over different time periods. Maybe Ms. Sweets will need to have her hair coiffed differently; perhaps wear wigs in some of her roles and vary her sensual come-ons. I don't know. I'm only good at imagining. I'm not a video production type person. But the key factor is that Ms. Sweets is a romantic, sensuous woman. She is compelling, charismatic, energetic, promiscuous, personable, and uninhibited. Sam thinks she'll be perfect.*

"He will showcase Ms. Sweets in every possible way over the many scenes. Oh, and that reminds me. Marty has a Monarch butterfly tattoo on her upper thighs. It borders her vagina; highlights it. Sam intends to incorporate Marty's trademark into all of Ms. Sweets' seduction scenes by hiring graphic animators to recreate that butterfly on every single film frame. It needs to flutter while Ms. Sweets makes love, like Rosemary describes Marty's lovemaking in her books. Sam believes the animated butterfly effect will create the most memorable films ever made; and the effect will make Ms. Sweets the greatest film sensation in history."

Frank: *"So, she becomes a part-time butterfly?"*

John: *"Something like that; but she'll be the butterfly you'll love, Frank."*

Frank: *"I need to read the Series' books. And I need to watch every one of Ms. Sweets' films. I want to discover what Sam sees in this woman."*

John: *"You'll not be disappointed. Her femininity will leave
you speechless. And her promiscuity will keep you awake
nights, pining for her."*

Frank: *"You think of her that much? Her hold on you is that
strong?"*

John: *"Yes and yes. I can't resist her; don't want to. Sam wanted
to watch the two of us playing. He's like that, you know."*

Frank: *"And she was……?"*

John: *"Into it. More than playfully into it. Casually immoral
and pleased with herself describes her some; but that
doesn't even begin to explain the effect she has on a man."*

Frank: *"On you, you mean? You're hooked? You love this girl?"*

John: *"Yes, hooked; but no, it's not possible to love her; not the
same way I love Mandy. It's different when I'm with Ms.
Sweets. It's not love. It's more like infatuation or an adoration thing, or submission to a goddess. I start feeling
this profound appreciation for her immorality; her total
absence of godliness. She kind of takes my mind away
from me; like I'll start imagining her naked, bounc-
ing up and down on a mattress with millions of dollars
showering down upon her to reward her for her joyous,
wanton promiscuity; or I'll imagine her surrounded by
a roomful of penises and I'm watching her, spellbound,
while she sucks and fucks every cock in the room; and
she's smiling and chortling and loving every moment of
it. It's her effervescent freedom from guilt and moralizing.
It's contagious."*

Frank: *"You make her sound like she's different from other
whores, John. But when you cut to the chase, they're all
just money grubbing cum dumpsters, aren't they?"*

John: *"Not exactly. When you get into Rosemary's books,
you'll understand them better. Different porn stars have*

different reasons for creating porn. Some do it strictly for the money. They don't put any more thought into it than that. Others do porn because they have psychological issues. They may like experiencing the feelings of dominance and submission; or they may want to take out their frustrations; others may want to experience voyeurism; others want to know how it feels to do it with different partners in different scene locations or in different homes; still others do it because they want to use porn to get revenge against former lovers, or as their venue for meeting new people. But with Ms. Sweets, it's none of those reasons."

Frank: *"What's Ms. Sweets' reason?"*

John: *"It's her happiness over being with a male's penis. That's it. That's all of it. She's infatuated with the male penis. I mean, she totally loves it. She adores the penis and does everything humanly possible to give every penis all the love that she can possibly give it. When you are with her, you'll understand that she cherishes the male penis; how she treasures her experiences with it; how she seems to be declaring to all who are watching her that she knows and appreciates that the penis is the source of life and her happiness. That's why men become smitten with her and obsessed over her sexuality.*

"She's Rosemary's Marty, the world's most notorious porn star. She's the unique, breathtakingly immoral intersection of freedom, beauty, promiscuity, and wealth. She says the exactly right things to a man at the right times while he's making love with her. For instance, she'll say:

'You feel so good inside me. I want you to cum inside me. I want you to give me all your cum. I want to feel your hot cum inside my pussy. I want to cum with you. Please,

let me have it. I need to feel it. My pussy is begging you for it.'

"She says lots of things like that. She gets her feelings into men's heads. That's why men have this overwhelming lust for her; why they want to hold her; kiss her; have coitus with her; hold fast to her and never let go of her. A completely different part of their brains takes over their lives and controls their actions. Shrinks call it the limbic effect. You'll see. You'll lose any sense of right or wrong. All you know is whatever Ms. Sweets wants, whatever pleases her, you must do. She'll put her sensuous branding iron against your mind; take ownership of your thoughts; and she'll corral you, along with her other devoted fans. When it pleases her, she will saddle you; and she'll ride you into erotic wonderland. You'll take her wherever she wishes to go; then she'll order you to do her bidding."

Frank: *"Like what?"*

John: *"Spend your money on her; drain your accounts; divorce your wife; commit murder; any and all of those things. You won't be able to help yourself. I know. Sex addiction is real. I never used to believe it, but it's true. It happens. It happened to me. I couldn't stay away from her. I fell on my sword for her. Whenever I was into Ms. Sweets, I was in heaven. I had to have her. A different part of my mind controlled me. Mandy didn't matter. Mandy fell out of the equation."*

Frank: *"Equation?"*

John: *"The moral equation. The weighing of rights and wrongs; the rationalizations of why you give in to temptation. It just wasn't there. The moral equation simply went 'Poof!' Right and wrong simply blew away. And then I was there, alone and intimate with Ms. Sweets. And nothing else mattered. My mind went away and I didn't care whether it ever came back to me."*

Frank: *"Do you think the same thing happened to Pete? Do you think he could have been so into Ms. Sweets that he killed Marge and the kids?"*

John: *"Yeah. Absolutely the same effect happened to him. Pete's an even bigger hound dog than I am. I'm sure he dove deeply into Ms. Sweets. I'm sure he even got hooked on her. But I'm just as sure that Pete did not kill Marge and their kids. I think there's an 'All Engines Stop' place in Pete's mind that he would never pass; kind of like a ship seeing an iceberg or a truck with failing brakes seeing a runaway truck ramp on a downhill mountain freeway. Especially with Pete. He'd go all engines back full and turn away. He'd take the off ramp. He's had far too much pussy in his life to let a porn star control his mind. Not our Pete."*

Frank: *"But there was a time when Moses came down from the mountain with his commandment tablets. And he saw the people had made a golden calf; and he took note of all their goings on. They had surrendered to debauchery. That's when he threw down the tablets and smashed them. Remember how the ground opened and the revelers that followed the ways of the golden calf got swallowed up into the earth? That story tells us there's one way or the other; that you can't have both. You can't have your cake and eat it, too. You can't just go back and forth between the two ways. So, what's to say Pete didn't go over to the immoral side and stay there?"*

John: *"Simple. Those events never happened. It's all just a pool filled with religious hogwash. All religions fill their followers' heads with those sorts of hogwash homilies. That's how religions keep people in their fold. Pete's the toughest of the tough; the strongest, most moral man among us. No woman could get him to toss away his family and religion."*

Frank: *"Not like Delilah made Samson ditch his people?"*

John: *"No, not Pete. This is our Pete, our Mench, we're talking about, for Christ's sake."*

Frank: *"Hope you're right. Anyway, I want to see this Ms. Sweets hottie. Joyce digs porn. She told me that your Mandy watches it, too. Let's say we all get together with our wives as these films are produced; and let's make a pact to see every one of them. You know, some goodies to get high on, combined with swaps and foursomes."*

John: *"You have a deal, my friend. Let's meet again tomorrow at the coffee shop across from the courthouse. Let's see our way through this murder case together, and let's be Pete's moral support. I'll get a private eye. We'll start our own investigation. By the time you've finished reading the Series, we'll get to the bottom of these murders. After the Series, there will definitely be a sequel to Pete's trial. He'll be a free man again.*

Frank: *"I just thought of something. It sounds like Sam's cousin and Sam will have enough material to keep Ms. Sweets creating sensational porn films for at least the next five years. Does Sam believe she'll be able to handle that much work? I mean, that's a great deal of fucking."*

John: *"And a great deal of acting as well. Remember, it will be filmed over several years. Sam needs to talk with her and see whether she's interested. But Sam wouldn't come up with a project like this if he didn't believe Ms. Sweets was the right woman to star in these roles. Sam's convinced himself that she's the one. He's declared her the unblinded, modern-day Eve with her fig leaf removed and her legs wide open.*

"Sam's version of Eve will put Ms. Sweets in charge of Eden's garden, not God. She won't be inclined to obey God's rules, only her own. And she won't be beholden to any Adam figure; nor interested in bearing Adam's children to multiply the human species. She'll only be interested in her own well-being, power, and pleasures. She'll be a committed whoring nympho; guiltless, through and through; and she'll love herself for whom she is. I agree with Sam. She'll be a film sensation. The fucking parts will be natural for her. She'll love every minute of performing every scene. Remember, Ms. Sweets has the 'It' factor.

Frank: *"But will she be able to handle the stardom? I'm asking about the paparazzi; the endless requests for her time from her premium members? Will she be able to resist the temptation of multi-millionaires and billionaires offering her marriage proposals? I mean, what if she quits in the middle of this?"*

John: *"I think that's why Sam is marrying her. It would be hard for her to walk away from eight billion dollars. Besides, she loves her work; loves creating her spellbinding porn; loves the different partners' personas; loves riding their cocks and all the different positions. She loves all that stimulation. And she loves the cocks and loves experiencing their penetration moments. It will be a never-ending journey of erotic exploration for her. It will be endless pleasure; her ultimate world. It's what she lives for. It will be fulfilling the greatest calling of her life. Sam is not the controlling type. He's the opposite of that. He loves her most when he knows she's enjoying herself. Sam will ensure that these porn films will be the greatest, most unforgettable ever created.*

"I know Sam. He'll challenge her and keep her interested. He'll make her porn sets magnificent. He'll help her find her perfect moods. He'll showcase her; ensure that she has the very best, premium porn partners with the most appealing penises; the best wardrobes, make-up artists; the best of everything; and the most attractive male movie stars and starlets creating the most exquisite porn with her. She'll be in romantic erotica heaven. Sam will treat her like the goddess she is. Not to worry!"

Frank: *"And this wedding is actually going to happen? Where, in some secret Mexican hide away; maybe some Las Vegas chapel? Do you know?"*

CHAPTER SEVEN

MARRYING PORNOGRAPHY

John: *"Yes. But it will not be in some hideaway or any marriage mill. It will be a huge extravaganza, broadcast live for all the world to witness. Sam told me all about it. You know Sam. He does nothing small. He's immensely proud of his new bride. He wants to glorify and reward her for being who she is. The wedding will venerate her and validate her exquisite pornography. It will promote her exceptional eroticism to the world; a wedding for the history books. Sam bought the Catholic Cathedral for it."*

Frank: *"You mean he rented it for a day?"*

John: *"No, I mean he bought it from the Archdiocese. Sam owns the cathedral now. He told me he is going to make their wedding symbolic. The wedding has another purpose besides Sam and Ms. Sweets tying the knot. He's removing the center aisle pews and installing a monstrously huge palanquin. It will have two gigantic California King sized beds raised up to eye level; supported by steel girders. It's wheels will be powered by little electric motors. It will move on twenty pneumatic air-filled rubber tires.*

"While the cathedral organ plays 'Here comes the bride,' Ms. Sweets will be positioned on a throne chair upon the California kings. She will be in her white bridal gown, performing her exquisite fellatio and breathtaking fornications with three of her porn partners, while the gigantic palanquin moves very slowly down the center aisle, newly enlarged to accommodate the palanquin. It will be a symbolic procession; a live porn show. It will signify traditional religion giving way to secular hedonism."

Frank: *"Blasphemy!"*

John: *"Yes, it will be right there, in your face, blasphemy. Pornography crushing religion; sweeping it away like an old, unwanted cobweb; replacing it with deification of the feminine vagina, just like the old Pagan temple worship practices before six thousand years ago. It will be the most glorious live porn show ever performed; and it will be televised for the world to see. It will mark the dawning of Modern Paganism; the advent of humanism.*

"Her procession to the altar will take the better part of an hour. She'll coax multiple ejaculations from her partners and have multiple orgasms herself while the organ plays soft religious themes, like 'Ave Maria,' and themes from 'The Credo.' After Sam and Ms. Sweets say their vows and become legally married, Sam wants to hear Mendelssohn's 'Wedding March' while he joins Ms. Sweets on the palanquin. He wants her to sit on his face so he can perform cunnilingus with her, while she performs fellatio with fresh penis partners. Then, he wants her to fornicate with them as her palanquin slowly rolls out of the cathedral. Sam wants Ms. Sweets and her pornography to be exalted. He wants the world's peoples to adore her as their divine, high priestess of porn; their new God. The entire

production will be filmed from all angles, of course. Sam intends to air it as the preview trailer for his eighteen porn film extravaganza.”

Frank: *“He's really going to do this?”*

John: *“Yes. He's told me that when he kisses his new bride, he wants her to have her partners' semen on her lips and flowing from her vagina. He wants to embrace her with one arm while he kisses her, while his other hand fingers her slippery wet vagina. Then, he wants to position her upon the altar and have her spread her gorgeous, shameless, welcoming legs while he kisses her insatiable, penis-craving pussy.”*

Frank: *“He truly does love her; especially her debaucheries, doesn't he”*

John: *“Yes. He's smitten. And his love transcends their age difference. He told me when the organ begins playing the ‘Wedding March,' he's going to cup his mouth to her vagina. That will be Sam's way of professing his love and adoration for her debauched lifestyle. It will be his way of sanctifying the glory of her pornography and all the liaisons that spring from it. It's a psychological form of love that joins her immoral soul to his immoral soul. Sam has always had disdain for the religion spewing moralizers.*

“Ms. Sweets is the perfect partner for Sam. Their minds, their belief systems are on the same page. They both think religious belief is on its way out. They would tell you that Asherah goddess worship dominated human belief systems from twenty thousand years ago until six thousand years ago. They'd tell you that the religious beliefs of the past six thousand years, those beliefs in an abstract God, are on its way out; and they are in the process of being replaced by a variation of the Asherah belief system.”

Frank: *"Which is our modern-day pornography with its highly acclaimed porn stars, right?"*

John: *"Exactly right. That's what makes this marriage about compatibility of beliefs. That's where Sam and Ms. Sweets are. That's heart to heart, soul to soul; lovers with like minds. That's what makes a marriage work. And that's what matters."*

Frank: *"So, Sam won't be troubled that she's off making porn; that she's away for a week or two at a time, having highly publicized romances with wealthy men, movie stars, and sports figures; and doing nightly escort sex with these men?"*

John: *"No, not at all. Sam will encourage her to be as promiscuous as she can possibly be. You see, his amygdala has flipped his mind's limbic switch to the permanently 'on' position. He loves her more every time she whores; and his love for her deepens with every porn film she creates. It's a perfect marriage for both of them. He'll champion her immorality in every way he possibly can. And the more notorious and profligate she is, the more Sam will love her. It's an opposite type of relationship from what most people have in their traditional marriages. Sam is thrilled beyond words to be married to the world's most notorious porn star. It's a new kind of love, Frank. It's more than accepting. It's supportive. It's encouraging and enabling. It's unrequitedly hedonistic, secular love. Sam believes porn is a socially acceptable life style now. He wants to promote it. He wants the world to accept it. He believes marrying Ms. Sweets will deliver the coup de gras to the concept of traditional marriages. And he very much wants to deliver the entire world to this woman and lay it at her feet. He's smitten.*

Frank: *"He's doing this wedding extravaganza to showcase her;
          to glorify her immorality; to make a statement, isn't he?
          I mean, afterward, at the reception, he'll likely be open
          to having the guests taking turns kissing her pussy, kiss-
          ing her while feeling her; fingering her while she's eating
          wedding cake; even fucking her; things like that, right? I
          mean, this whole wedding gig is about the world taking
          off on a whole new societal trajectory. It's about exalting
          immorality; making it socially normal and acceptable;
          lifting it up; honoring it; and helping it take off, isn't it?"*

John: *"Yes Frank. It is. The world is changing."*

Frank: *"John, I just thought of something. You said this Ms. Sweets
          woman has the angelic face of the Madonna. You told me
          how immoral she is. And you told me how she's going to
          be playing this murderess character in the Secret Butter-
          fly Series™. Well, what's to say she didn't fall in love with
          Pete, instead of the other way around? I mean what if she
          wanted Pete, but Marge and the kids got in her way? What
          if she's one of those people who can't tell whether she's act-
          ing or whether she's doing murders in real life? I mean, if
          she's so immoral about everything else in her life, what was
          to stop her from murdering Marge and the kids?"*

John: *"That's crazy. She's a woman. They don't commit murders.
          Besides, how would she get rid of the bodies?"*

Frank: *"Some women murder, John. You also said you fell on
          your sword for her. What's to say that one of her porn
          partners, or lovers, wouldn't do her bidding for her? You
          also said she's irresistible. Don't you think a woman like
          that could get a man do her dirty work for her?"*

John: *"Well, maybe. You might have something there, especially
          the way the family was murdered by a hunting knife with
          a serrated edge. Now you've got me wondering."*

Frank: *"They were murdered by a knife? Are you sure it was a knife? How would you know that? Aren't the police are still searching for the murder weapon?"*

John: *"Sam read the police report. I don't know how he got the report, but he did. He told me how they were murdered. Ghastly, like their necks were nearly sawed through. It took a man's strength. Sam was being cautious. He concluded it couldn't have been Ms. Sweets. I personally never suspected her. I had already ruled her out. Her face just looks too innocent. She's so sweet and charming. I couldn't imagine it."*

Frank: *"Then who?"*

John: *"I have no idea, honestly. But it wasn't her."*

Frank: *"Agreed. It had to be a man. Hell, she was probably fucking Pete while his family was being murdered."*

John: *"That's what Sam believes."*

Frank: *"Wow, if Pete was with Ms. Sweets, the police have everything all wrong. Anyway, that's why we'll hire your private eye friend, right?"*

John: *"Right."*

PREVIEW

From THE BUTTERFLY YOU LOVE©:

'I was six then; David was there, too. I think his parents expected he'd want to play with me; but he didn't want to. David walked around with a magnifying glass, looking for ants and burning them by focusing the sunlight on them. Marvin, his father, told him to stop doing that. David didn't listen. He kept burning ants. Then, Marvin took the magnifying glass away from David. David ran down the yard; then he walked onto the driveway looking for ants. Whenever he saw an ant, he stomped on it and yelled "Die, ant! Die!" He was cursing at the ants. Marvin told him to stop that, too.

'Then, David went somewhere. He was gone for a short while; but when he came back, he had some firecrackers and he returned to the driveway. He found some little ant hills beside the driveway, where those little red ants lived. Then he set off firecrackers in those little ant hills. He laughed like a crazy person while he blew up those ants. Again, he screamed: "Die ants! Die!" Even at my young age, I remember thinking there was something wrong with David. The way he kept going after those innocent, defenseless ants, like he was obsessively compelled to murder every ant in the world. He just didn't seem normal to me . . . . Chapter One.

The portrait expressed her feeling perfectly. She wore her special smile, the one that comes when everything is right. Her face was confident and content, combined with her mischievous hint of victory glow. She radiated her heart's happiness from that smile because she was on top of the world that day. Bob had achieved his breakthrough in their love making that afternoon. He had softly kissed her between her wings for that first time and become smitten by the tastes of her lady flower. His face told her that he had experienced reverence and wonderment; his smile assured her that he loved it; that he felt more connected to her than ever; and that he loved her. The portrait captured that instant when she knew she'd stolen his love away from Barbara.. . . . . .Chapter Two.

"No Ed, listen to me. I'm serious. Her hair was not black hair like people get from black ancestors. She didn't have that kind of black hair. It was not coarse, thick black hair, and it didn't have any trace of kinky curl either. It wasn't that deep inky black color like dark peoples' hair. It was that soft, lustrous off-black; brownish; thin-strand, fine silky hair that Jewish women have. That girl had a beautiful, delicate, Jewish fineness about her hair; and her face. She had a beautiful, porcelain, doll-like face, Ed; like a Jewish girl's face. I recognized her hair immediately, Ed. It's the kind of soft, fine hair a woman touches over a man's face and body while she makes love with him. It's soft delicate hair; and it's silky lustrous, too. It's the kind of sensuous hair that turns men on and drives them crazy. I know it does. And that reddish streak draws men's attention to her hair and face. It's very noticeable. It draws you right into her eyes. That face will attract men, Ed. She's got the kind of face that men dream about kissing. And, did you notice her eyes? They were slightly widely set; like her mother's; but they had those soft brown pools that invite men to dive into them and fall in love. Those are Jewish eyes, Ed. I

know what I saw. I'm telling you, Ed, Trudy's roommate has a Jewish bloodline. I'm positive." . . . . Chapter Four.

'You're a lovely, immoral whore; and I adore you,' his imagination said. 'May I do what I've dreamed of doing since I first saw you?'

'Of course, you may. I was hoping you'd ask,' his fascination heard her reply . . . . Chapter Four.

"Fuck off, Bitch!" There, Marty had said it, while looking directly at Mrs. Raybenald's startled face. The swim coach's eyes registered disbelief. A long pause followed while the two antagonists surveyed each other . . . . Chapter Six.

It was a little thing. The adults seemed to pass it off as a simple oddity to be quickly forgotten; but to a little girl who had just lost her daddy, and been whisked away to a boarding school two thousand miles from home, it was very significant . . . Chapter Seven.

I think they do it with each other, without needing a boy to do it. But I don't want to ask them about it. They scare me. I'm afraid to be friends with them. They'd want me to be like them. I don't think I'm like them. I think I want to do it with boys. I don't know." . . . . Chapter Nine.

"I'm okay, Maria, Ohhh, Heee, Heee, Ohhh, Billy, Donny, that tickles. I feel my clit swelling. It's wonderful. I'm getting all wet inside." . . . . Chapter Ten.

"Then you'd better jump, fat ass. Damn you!" shouted Mrs. Raybenald as she bended down to pick up a second life ring. *The woman had lost control of rational reason. "I'm going to throw another one at you, fat ass. I'll keep throwing them at you, until I*

hit you and knock you off. Either way, you are going into the water! So, you'd better jump! Jump! Damn you! Jump!" Mrs. Raybenald screamed. . . . . .Chapter Eleven.

"Your bullying needs to stop." . . . . .Chapter Eleven.

'I'm leaving. I'm going away for a long time; forever. I'm going where I'm going to get away from the two of you. Okay? I don't want either of you in my life anymore. I hope you will finally understand what I have been trying to tell you for many years. Not that either of you care, but I'm going to a very special place where everybody can do a perfect butterfly and where everybody loves everybody else. I am determined that, for once in my life, I will finally do a perfect butterfly. You will both know that despite your best efforts you were not able to defeat my spirit. I'm going to show you. You'll see.'

> *Love,*
> *Maria, your perfect butterfly,'* . . . . Chapter Twelve.

'I love you, Marty. I very sincerely hope that you love me too. I believe that you did love me. I believe that you are the only person that has ever loved me. I hope you will always remember me as the fat girl who finally did a perfect butterfly. I hope I'll always be 'The Butterfly You Love.'

With all the love that I can give you,
Maria.' . . . . Chapter Twelve.

'Why did I get stuck with an asshole for a mother? Why won't Dad see what she's done to me? Why must I be the chunky fat girl; the one cursed with a double chin? Why couldn't I have a sleek racehorse, come ride me, come fuck me, body like Marty has? I am so alone, so

afraid; but I am not afraid of dying! Hell no! I am afraid of living! I want no part of it. No more! No more ridicule; no more trying to hide my body in baggy clothes; no more hearing snickers behind my back. I'm too good for this shit life. I want out of it. I will do one final butterfly. I'll show them what they did to me. Fuck them! Fuck everybody! I am leaving all of you. I'm done.' . . . . Chapter Twelve.

'She's totally naked. How did she get in here? And how did she end up this way? And what does she have in her hands? And why are her legs all taped up like that? Was someone trying to kill her?' Then he realized that Maria wasn't moving. His shock and curiosity turned to fright. He ran to her in a panic. "What the hell have you done?" he shouted aloud at the still body.. . . . . Chapter Twelve.

'Miss Shameless told me there was nothing wrong with doing that. Miss Iniquity told me Mommy had it coming; and Miss Promiscuity told me I should get Daddy alone, away from Mommy; then kiss him until he loved me more than Mommy.' . . . . . Chapter Thirteen.

"I intend to be a promiscuous, shameless, iniquitous, immoral, loving woman." . . . . Chapter Thirteen.

"Slim's excited about it. It's a fucking monster, right on top of a trap dome, high in the Bakken Shale. Slim just has a nose for finding oil. We've leased a shit load of acres around it. Slim's had land men all over the area buying acres while he kept it tight holed before word got out, and he's moved six of our deep rigs out of Colorado's DJ basin up to North Dakota." . . . . .Chapter Fourteen.

Marge had thoughtfully run the numbers, like smart housewives do. Ed had insurance with an accidental death benefit that paid double. Those numbers helped her see him in a whole new way. Dead by accident, Ed's corpse was worth six million. But if he died naturally, she'd only get three million; and she'd wait until she was too old to enjoy it. . . . . .Chapter Fifteen.

'He's asked me twice before to tell him how I did that perfect murder. He's dying to know how I did it. My murders fascinate David, especially that one.'. . . . . Chapter Fifteen.

'Carl surprised me right there in the cabin's kitchen. He came up behind me, locked his huge arm around my waist and peeled down my panties. I became instantly wet. My clitoris ballooned. My vagina has a sense for Carl. It's our body chemistry thing. I totally love fucking him. Fire flames rushed through my blood. I wanted him instantly; had to feel him inside me. It's like that with Carl. Always spontaneous. Always heavenly. Always never enough. Always, I want to continue fucking him forever. He entered me from behind while he continued kissing my neck.' . . . . Chapter Fifteen.

'When Darren came inside me that first time, while Carol cried and screamed like she was losing her mind, while begging him to stop, I felt in total control of him and her.' . . . . Chapter Fifteen.

"No, it's not. It's close, but it is not my ultimate feeling. That only happens in the murder cavern, with its enormously high ceiling, recessed lights, and sound system that surrounds the entire chamber. It happens after I've performed one of my murders; after I've peeled off all my silks and my panties; after I've been psyched by the strobe lights.". . . . . Chapter Fifteen.

"So, by killing my fetus, I am not killing its soul. Its soul will go on to its next life. It's present life is cut short; but that's all. Look, Miss Promiscuity, when I was a pagan temple goddess, we thought nothing of impaling unwanted babies and children with our swords; then throwing them into the fire. We didn't have long discussions or guilt trips over doing what was necessary." . . . . Chapter Fifteen.

"I feel connected to David, like he's family, somehow. He helps me feel good about myself. He knows our murders are therapeutic for my mental health; and that I must continue performing them. He and I are of like minds. That's why it's so hard for me to leave him." . . . . Chapter Fifteen.

"But your girlfriend butterflies? You said you talk with them?" . . . . *Chapter Fifteen.*

"Seeing men in pain helped Patty have her orgasms. Giving men pain was something she simply had to do, to make herself feel like a complete, total woman." . . . . Chapter Fifteen.

"That's what's causing a conflict for me. I feel this deep need to go to David; to have David close to me in my human life, like he's my destiny or something like that. There's a certain unspoken realism about me and David. It's like David, alone, has this profoundly deep understanding about my emotional needs. I'm drawn toward that understanding, like my butterfly soul is called to migrate. His understanding of my needs enables David and me to commit our murders, together." . . . . Chapter Fifteen.

"I've decided to murder Barbara, Bob. I know she's your closest friend; but it's not healthy for a man to have his feelings divided between two women." . . . . Chapter Fifteen.

"*Remember the way we were, Bob, when I was the high priestess of Baalbek? Remember how we enslaved the Gobekli Tepe tribes to build my altar atop my temple's eight-hundred-ton stones? Remember how splendidly I fornicated? Wasn't it wonderful hearing our entire tribe cheer for me while I impaled the children of the non-believers and shoved them into the fire?*" . . . . Chapter Fifteen.

"*David often quotes Cato, that Roman Senator who ended his speeches by saying: 'Carthage must be destroyed!' Cato didn't want Rome to have any competition from Carthage, even though Rome had already defeated Carthage in the first two Punic Wars. I will not tolerate competition from Barbara. She is Carthage. I am Rome. I defeated her by taking Bob from her. And now I must destroy her. Like Rome obliterated Carthage in the third Punic War, I must also obliterate Barbara. Like Rome erased the existence of Carthage from the world, I must erase Barbara's existence from the world. I must do as David says.*". . . . . Chapter Fifteen.

"*I'm thinking fire; probably electrical. I want to burn the bitch. Maybe I'll fake an accident with the Blather-Flameer. It shorts out a lot.*". . . . . Chapter Fifteen.

"*Stand with me, Bob. Stand by my side, always. Tell me you love my lovemaking and how my mind works, Bob. I need you to appreciate how hard I've worked to create my exquisite films and all the scenes I've done to advanced my porn career. Tell me you're proud that I've freed myself from morality and inhibition; and how much you love watching me perform my explicit erotica. That's what I live for.*". . . . . Chapter Fifteen.

More to come.

Hello dear readers and listeners. I'm Melanie Monarch, your audiobook reader. I'll be narrating the SECRET BUTTERFLY SERIES ™ for your listening pleasure. A fascinating young woman is beginning her life's quest to discover the true nature of love. Her name is Marty. Let me introduce her to you while I narrate THE BUTTERFLY YOU LOVE ©, the first book of our Series.

THE BUTTERFLY YOU LOVE MAY BE PURCHASED OR ORDERED WHEREVER BOOKS ARE SOLD:

TO ORDER THE BUTTERFLY YOU LOVE:

ISBN-13 978-0-9982321-5-7 for eBook
ISBN-13 978-0-9982321-6-4 for Paperback

Hello readers and listeners, I'm Melanie Monarch, your audio book narrator. Won't you please come and flutter along with m I invite you to join me on an unforgettable journey of erotic romances, intrigue, provocative new thoughts; and, gasp, murder. Let's begin with THE BUTTERFLY YOU LOVE™. It's the first book of our audiobooks from the SECRET BUTTERFLY SERIES™.